Her captor sat in profile....

His face was gray in the dusky light of the car, his eyes shadowed but hard and focused. "How long can you go without sleep?" Bitsy asked him.

"As long as it's necessary."

"How do you do it?" she asked. "Do they train you guys? Put you through some secret agent boot camp complete with decoder rings and days of physical and mental deprivation until you're an elite spy machine?"

He pulled into a gas station and turned off the car. When he reached for the keys, her hand reached for him, her fingertips moving lightly across his skin. Her lips parted, inviting him in.

"Is that what you are, Mick? A machine?" Her fingers were at the back of his neck now.

Foolish, he thought, even as his head lowered to her in response. *Wrong.* Then his mouth found hers and there was no thought. Only heat. Desire. Hunger.

In his kiss, Bitsy was falling, swept away by sensation and an overwhelming dominant male sexuality she had never experienced before. When he pulled away, she was bereft.

He held her gaze, desire in the hot blue of his eyes. "Does that answer your question?"

SYDNEY RYAN

HIGH-HEELED ALIBI

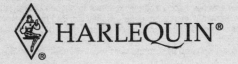

HARLEQUIN®

TORONTO • NEW YORK • LONDON
AMSTERDAM • PARIS • SYDNEY • HAMBURG
STOCKHOLM • ATHENS • TOKYO • MILAN • MADRID
PRAGUE • WARSAW • BUDAPEST • AUCKLAND

ISBN 0-373-22919-4

HIGH-HEELED ALIBI

Printed in U.S.A.

ABOUT THE AUTHOR

A native of New York, Sydney Ryan graduated magna cum laude from Syracuse University with a degree in public communications. She worked in a variety of fields, including telecommunications and public relations, before devoting herself full-time to fiction writing.

She lives happily ever after in upstate New York with her husband, Jim, and their two teenage children, J.J. and Ariana.

Books by Sydney Ryan

HARLEQUIN INTRIGUE
919—HIGH-HEELED ALIBI

Don't miss any of our special offers. Write to us at the following address for information on our newest releases.

Harlequin Reader Service
U.S.: 3010 Walden Ave., P.O. Box 1325, Buffalo, NY 14269
Canadian: P.O. Box 609, Fort Erie, Ont. L2A 5X3

CAST OF CHARACTERS

Bitsy Leigh—After her marriage self-destructed, she'd fled the fast lane and found sanctuary in her small California hometown and a job in her uncle's mortuary. Until one night the stormy baby blues of a six-foot-two-inch stiff winked at her, telling her he wasn't dead yet... and neither was she.

Mick James—The undercover agent was a dead man. Or so everyone thought when he was set up to take the fall for an assassination attempt. Only a scalpel-wielding beauty named Bitsy could prove his innocence. But would he find anyone to believe her before his enemies find them?

Radley Kittredge—Insiders said the popular San Francisco congressman was the real deal— a politician who cared deeply about his constituents. But if it weren't for a brave valet stepping between him and a killer's bullet, Kittredge's career...and life... would have been over.

Arthur Prescott—A believer that everyone deserves a chance, the top operative had turned Mick's life around twelve years ago when he'd recruited him for The Agency. Now he'd arrived from Central Headquarters to give Mick another chance...one final time.

Grey Torre—One of California's most successful divorce lawyers, his skill at securing his female clients generous settlements had earned him the nickname the Spago Ladies' lawyer, but he'd handled his childhood friend Bitsy's divorce from Johnny Dumont and his millions for free. Could he save his favorite damsel in distress this time when she was taken hostage by an apparent madman?

Chapter One

God, even the man's feet were beautiful.

And Bitsy had seen enough bare feet to know they should've been, at least, unsightly. At a minimum, amusing. These feet, though, stuck out beneath the sheet like a final curtain call, naked, proud, without wrinkles, thickened, yellowed skin pads or oddly crooked toes. Smooth, sculpted, these feet did not reveal the many miles walked, only the fine-grained desire of many miles more wished for.

At the ankles, a white cloth began and spread wide and long across a large, unmoving body.

Above was the face, tanned and crowned by a bleached cap of hair. A small circular scar puckered the skin above the right collarbone, saving the man from total perfection. Otherwise, the jawline was not too square, not too soft. The lips tipped at the corners, teasing. The dark brows arched, then dipped deep toward the nose, finishing the face with an air of "to hell with you." The eyes were closed, but they had to be blue, the blue of night secrets.

Bitsy stared at the man, following his features one by one and thinking of dreams she'd had not so long ago.

The man was beautiful.

Beautiful and dead.

She turned away, clicking her tongue against her teeth in a dismissive note. The sound echoed across the silent room, the gurgling and whirring of the taps turned off for the night. Emotion had no place here. An occasional retching was allowed. Obligatory solemnness was expected. But emotional control was the cornerstone of the profession. And what had called her to her current circumstance.

She snapped on one pair of latex gloves from a waiting wheeled table, and then another. She stepped back, surveying the still figure on the metal stretcher. He must've just arrived. The skin was supple. The deceptive flush of life had only begun to pale. The eyes would require blue stipple work around the lids. The right lid had opened a crack in the inside corner, but a pinch of cream worked underneath, then firmed with Number 6, would take care of the problem. Of course, the head would incline slightly to put the carotid suture in shadow.

She stepped closer, drawing back the sheet at the neck, looking for the suture. When Uncle Nelson had suggested her cosmetology training would be useful in the family business, she knew it was exactly the type of work she'd been looking for. Few people understood her choice. Their reactions ran from macabre fascination to hardly concealed repulsion. It didn't bother her. She'd come home, seeking peace and quiet. At the moment, she only asked from life no more surprises. People could say whatever they wanted about her job, but one thing was certain. There were no surprises.

Bitsy looked up. Two blue eyes looked back at her.

Shock threw her body back. The cart she slammed into skittered across the room. Instruments clattered to the floor. The eyes, the exact shade she'd imagined, blinked.

She backed away, her hands reaching behind her, patting the air, searching for something solid to grasp and support her. Even above the room's always bitter odor, she could smell her shameful scent of fear.

Control. Her mind repeated the command, seeking to quiet her racing heart.

The eyes staring up at her blinked again, slowly, like a newborn babe.

Spasmodic muscle contracture. It was not uncommon in corpses. Some had been known to rise right up in their caskets. As if to prove her point, the body before her sat up.

She found the counter, fought to stay standing. The sheet fell away from the man's upper torso, revealing a bronzed span of muscled chest. Frantic fear beat against Bitsy's breastbone. Her mouth opened in a silent protest as her mind moved into overdrive, attempting to calm her. *Okay, okay. Major cadaveric spasm.* She gripped the counter's sharp edge.

The corpse's gaze narrowed, focusing. He rubbed his forehead. Closing his eyes against the harsh overhead light, he moaned. Bitsy ran out of rational explanations.

"You're dead." Her held breath whooshed out with the words.

The man squinted one eye open, letting out another soft groan. His body shuddered at the room's cool temperature. His nose sniffed the chemical smell. Shielding his eyes with one hand, he gave Bitsy a thorough once-over. She pulled tight the lab jacket she'd slipped on against the room's coolness, but her leather miniskirt and fishnet stockings were still visible. She watched the man's gaze lift to take in her skull earrings, the white foundation, black lipstick, her hair dyed jet-black and streaked with silver.

He wet his lips and swallowed as if his mouth were dry. His voice came out a croak. "Something tells me this isn't the Pearly Gates."

"This is Memorial Manor," she said with as much dignity as possible for someone with a bride of Frankenstein beehive. She'd been dressing when the phone had rung. Gwen's son had tripped over the shreds of his mummy costume and needed stitches. Could Bitsy fill in at the funeral home for a few hours? Uncle Nelson never left it unattended on Halloween. Bitsy had zipped a skirt over her bodysuit and fishnet stockings and rushed right over.

The man massaged his forehead. His hands were broad, big-knuckled. "What's Memorial Manor? A halfway house to heaven?" His speech was thick. He paused to wet his lips again. "Your people must not have talked to my many fans. They'd definitely have me first in line to fire and damnation."

"You're not dead."

The man's mouth lazily lifted at one corner. "That's a relief. Now, maybe you could tell me where the hell… sorry, poor choice of words. Where am I exactly?"

"Memorial Manor is a funeral home."

The man pointed a finger at her. "But you said I'm not dead."

"You were," she tried to explain. "Now, you're not."

"Either I'm dead…" The man swung his long legs across the narrow gutter on the side of the gurney. "…or I'm not." He stood up quickly as if needing the floor's firmness beneath his feet. The sheet almost slipped away from his body. Before he caught it, Bitsy endured a vision of golden maleness.

She averted her head. "Believe me, you're alive."

"Thanks for the vote of confidence. Now, explain to me what I'm doing here and how I got here?"

The slur was gone. He spoke with the strength that defined him physically. Bitsy looked back, relieved to see the sheet securely gathered and tucked in tight at his waist. "There must've been a mistake."

He arched one brow.

"A big mistake," she offered.

He studied her with keen, assessing eyes. "You work here?"

She nodded. Her skull earrings swayed.

"And your job title would be?"

She went for a delicate laugh. "Haven't you ever seen Vera the Vampire Vixen before?"

"No. And yet until now, I believed I'd lived a full life, which, according to you, I'm about to continue."

"Heck, I saw three of them tonight already on my way here from the house. Vampire vixens were more popular than I expected this year."

The man kneaded his forehead as if warding off a migraine. "Who would've guessed?"

"I'll admit we do get carried away, but around here, Halloween is like a national holiday."

The man stopped rubbing his brow. "And where exactly is 'around here'?"

"Canaan, California."

The man still looked blank.

"About twenty miles south of San Francisco," Bitsy explained. "The City of Death."

"The City of Death?" the man repeated.

Bitsy nodded. Her skull earrings swung. "We've got seventeen cemeteries, one million corpses and a funeral home on almost every corner. We've got more famous residents here than Los Angeles—except ours are all dead."

The man looked at her as if waiting for the punch line.

"Tina Turner's dog was buried in a fur coat at the Pets Rest Cemetery."

The other corner of the man's mouth quirked, his smile complete. And devastating. "It's Halloween. I'm in Canaan, California, City of Death," he repeated. He studied her, his large palm still shading his face, making the angled lines longer, bolder. "You're a mortician?"

"Restorative artist," she corrected.

The man stared at her a second more before breaking into a spontaneous laugh, his teeth flashing white. Something seized inside Bitsy and tightened. Yearnings remembered, desires denied. She smiled back tentatively. Alive, the man was deadly.

"Okay, what am I doing here?" His laughter stopped.

Bitsy's hesitant smile remained. "The report of your demise is greatly exaggerated?"

Clutching the sheet at his waist, the man began to pace, sidestepping the large drain in the middle. Despite his size, he moved with an unanticipated grace. He stopped and aimed a finger at her. Bitsy pressed tighter to the counter.

"Let's go over this once more. You're Vera the Vampire Vixen." His finger jabbed his bare chest. "I'm Lazarus." His one hand clutched the sheet while the other panned the room. "And this is Memorial Manor, where they obviously strive to put the 'fun' in funeral."

Unable to give the man the logical explanation he

demanded, Bitsy said nothing. The slim glint of a scalpel on the floor near him caught her attention. She took a sideways step toward the instrument fallen from the cart. She was sure there was a reason for what had happened, and the man seemed harmless…but bottom line, he was a man. A half-naked, very alive man. It was more than enough of a combination to make Bitsy wary.

She inched her body along the counter, closer to the scalpel.

"And tonight's Halloween," the man continued.

"Trick or…" She slid her foot toward the knife.

"Treat," the man finished as he swooped down and snatched the scalpel. Bitsy jerked her head up and met the man's dark-blue eyes.

He tested the blade with the pad of his thumb. Her breath stilled, a dreaded helplessness coming over her. The silence was long, magnifying their aloneness. As Gwen had called over her shoulder as she'd hurried out the door earlier, "It should be nice and quiet until I get back. There's only you and one in the icebox."

The "one in the icebox" looked at her now as his thumb rhythmically smoothed across the edge of the scalpel.

She thought of Gwen, the sudden emergency, the too obviously gorgeous corpse. Halloween. Comprehension came, along with relief and annoyance as Bitsy realized exactly what was going on.

Trick or treat.

"Give me that." She seized the instrument so

quickly the man didn't have time to react. "It'll have to be sterilized." She aimed the knife at his chest. "Lanie put you up to this, didn't she?"

"Excuse me?" To his credit, the man was convincingly confused.

"And Gwen is in on it, too, isn't she?" Bitsy jabbed the knife in the air, underscoring her words.

"Who's Lanie? Who's Gwen?"

"You know damn—" Bitsy stopped. Giving up swearing was part of her control program. Besides, she wasn't mad at the man. He was probably one of the many out-of-work actors who came to California like lambs to the slaughter. She couldn't blame him for taking advantage of an opportunity to make a few easy bucks. She hoped he'd charged Lanie a small fortune.

"You know." She gave the space between them a stab with the scalpel. "All I'm trying to do is lead a nice, normal life, but that cousin of mine can't let things be."

The man's gaze scanned the room and returned to Bitsy. "This is normal?"

She ignored his comment. "Tell me this. What's the crime in waking each morning, working each day, going to bed each night…alone?" The scalpel punctured the air again.

The man took a step back. "Thousands of people do it every day."

"Exactly," she agreed with an approving flourish of the scalpel. "Thousands, millions, gazillions. Is there anything wrong if I'm one of them?"

"Is there?" The man repeated.

Her voice dropped. "I've known passion. I have." She leaned in toward the man. "Believe me, I've ridden that roller coaster."

The man stared back at her. "Three minutes of thrills? Thirty minutes of wanting to throw up?"

Bitsy smiled, her frustration deflated. She slipped the scalpel into the lab jacket's pocket and held out her hand. "Bitsy Leigh, currently crazed, but, on a good day, calm, controlled cosmetician and upstanding citizen of Canaan."

The half-naked man took her hand. The charming smile returned. "Bitsy? Is that short for something?"

"Momma said it was supposed to be Betsy but Daddy didn't put on his glasses when he filled out the hospital paperwork. Daddy always joked it could've been worse. Batsy or Bootsy or, God forgive, Buttsy."

The man studied her a second as if trying to decide if she was putting him on. He made his decision and broke into a low laugh, his hand still holding hers, his skin warm. Bitsy liked the silvery sound of his laughter tempering the room's many edges. Her hand stayed in his.

"What is—" As she started to ask his name, the sound of a car pulling into the upper parking lot stopped her. She dropped the man's hand. "I'll bet that's Lanie and her partner in crime, Gwen. Okay, ladies, now it's your turn for a little trick or treat." She marched toward the door.

"Bitsy?" The man called after her.

She turned, a finger to her lips. "Stay right here. Don't make a sound. I'll pay you half the amount you charged Lanie."

She was gone before he could stop her. He crossed the room and stepped out into the hall to follow her when, from behind, he heard the whispered summons:

"Michael."

BITSY STRODE PAST THE ROOMS of tile and porcelain, linoleum and chromium steel to the stairs. The main floor was pickled oak, chintz, spongy carpet and muted lighting. The knocker sounded twice at the front door. She crossed the reception area that always smelled of cedar and opened one of the wide, carved double doors. Two policemen stood in the perpetual soft glow of the entryway. One officer was tall, dark, Latino. His partner was older, bald, short and fleshy. They eagle-eyed her attire. The older policeman commented with an abrupt grunt.

Bitsy folded her arms so that the lab jacket covered the top of her leopard-print bodysuit and tipped back her head in appraisal. She definitely had to give Lanie and Gwen an A for effort. She nodded approval. "I'll bet you guys didn't have an easy time renting authentic-looking costumes on Halloween?"

The taller cop's brow furrowed.

"Nice touch." Bitsy tapped the badge pinned on

his chest. Both policemen pulled back. The young cop rested his hand on his holster.

"Ma'am, we're canvassing the area in response to a bulletin the station received earlier."

"Excuse me just a minute." Bitsy wiggled between the two men to the generous, curved porch and leaned over its railing. She peered left and right, looking for her cousin and Gwen snickering somewhere in the shrubs lining the circular drive. The bushes were still, their evergreen gone black in the night.

"Ma'am?" The tall officer attempted again, his voice thinner.

She turned to the men. Their faces solemn, they were obviously intent on carrying out this charade to its conclusion. She stepped between them and paused at the door. Might as well give Lanie her money's worth. She gestured for the men to enter.

The partners glanced at each other. "After you," the tall one insisted to Bitsy. The two men followed her into the foyer, where she shut the door and faced them. Clasping her hands in front of her chest, she spoke in the hushed tones generated by the surroundings. "How can I help you?"

"Ma'am, as I was saying," the tall cop tried again, "we received an APB earlier this evening about a man named Michael James—"

She nodded comprehension. "I have him ready for you."

"He's here?" The short cop finally spoke.

Bitsy's expression stayed somber. "I don't mean to be indelicate, gentlemen, but he's not exactly going anywhere now, is he?"

The puzzled look between the policemen continued much longer this time.

"I'll get him for you," she offered and turned toward the hall.

"Ma'am, we'll go with you. We don't want anyone hurt."

She stopped beside a crushed-velvet sofa and faced them. "How thoughtful, Officer." Her voice was as smooth as the short officer's hairless dome. "But cremains are as light as a feather."

"Cremains?" the bald cop blurted.

Bitsy fought a smile. She cast her gaze downward as if in contemplation. "There is one problem. Usually by the time the cremains are released, the family has chosen an appropriate urn."

"What does she mean cremains?" the same cop demanded.

"But not to worry. We do have the ever-efficient double-layered brown bag. Let me check if the cremains have cooled and gone through the blender." She stepped briskly toward the hall.

"Cremains, Hector?" the cop questioned his partner. Bitsy allowed herself a smile.

But when she turned back, her features were respectfully pious. "Gentlemen, I understand. We're all professionals. Yet, no matter how many times our chosen paths bring us face-to-face with death, it's difficult to think of anyone, even a stranger, as anything but brimming with life."

"Hector," the cop said out of the side of his mouth, "what the hell is this broad talking about?"

Hector made a shushing motion with his hand. The other hand still rested on his holster. "Ma'am, are you telling us the man we're looking for is dead?"

Bitsy smiled patiently as her upturned palm made a semicircle. "Look around you, gentlemen. You wouldn't exactly come here looking for a live body."

"What we came looking for," Hector said, "was a man, early thirties, blond, about six foot two, two hundred-ten pounds, athletic build."

Bitsy crossed herself. "May he rest in peace."

Hector attempted to understand. "You're saying this man—

"The dearly departed." She couldn't resist.

"The dearly departed," the cop repeated through thin lips, "was cremated?"

Bitsy raised her hands, steepled her fingers and closed her eyes. "Ashes to ashes, dust to dust." She opened her eyes to the men's wonderfully confounded expressions. "Is there a problem, officers? That is the man you came here looking for, isn't it?"

She had planned to let the "policemen" squirm until they could report to Lanie this little glitch in her plan, but the two men looked so bewildered, she didn't have the heart to prolong their suffering. She might as well tell them now that she had caught on to her cousin and Gwen's questionably funny Halloween prank before the men had even knocked on the front door.

"Did the APB say the suspect was dead?" The short cop demanded of his partner.

"Okay, guys, you can give it up," Bitsy interjected. She would tell them the truth, go get Michael James or whatever his name was with his heart still steadily beating, and they could all be on their way to her cousin's boyfriend's costume party.

"It said possibly armed and dangerous. It didn't say possibly armed and dead," Hector said disgustedly. "It wouldn't surprise me if those SFPD desk jockeys got their wires crossed and sent us out on a manhunt for a corpse."

Bitsy felt a first frisson of doubt. "Fellas, it's okay," she assured them. "I know what's going on."

"I'm glad someone does," Hector said. "All I know is earlier this evening, we received an all-points bulletin from the San Francisco Police Department telling us to comb the area for a fugitive possibly headed for this locale."

The short cop snorted. "I'll tell you exactly what's going on. They didn't want to send a car to claim the body. I say we FedEx this poor bum's ashes right to the commissioner."

"A fugitive?" Bitsy's skepticism echoed off the dark paneled walls. "Possibly armed and dangerous?"

The older cop huffed another disgusted breath. "Not any longer."

Bitsy studied the two men. She slowly smiled. "You guys are good. For a moment, you almost had me believing you're real cops."

Hector looked down at her. "Ma'am," he said, pointing to the patch on his shirtsleeve. "We're members of the Canaan City Police Department."

Bitsy stared at the colored patch, her smile dissolving. At one of the courses she'd taken on self-defense, she'd learned crimes were often committed by assailants posing as policemen. Uniforms, security badges and guns were easy to obtain. There was one way, however, to determine if someone was really a legitimate member of the police force: their uniforms would have departmental-issued patches on the upper sleeve. These patches could not be duplicated. Her gaze met Hector's.

"You guys are real cops?"

"Ma'am, that's what we've been trying to tell you."

She didn't wait to hear more. She turned and ran down the stairs, past the chrome and linoleum rooms, ignoring the policemen's shouts to stop until she came to the room where the "corpse" had been. She stopped in the entryway, panting.

The room was empty.

She spun around and faced the police right behind her. "He's gone!"

"Yes." The short one nodded. "Dearly departed."

She shook her head. "He's not dead."

Again a long, puzzled look passed between the partners. "Ma'am," Hector began.

"Shh! Did you hear that?" Bitsy looked to the stairs. Above them was the sound of footsteps crossing the oak floor.

"Inside." Hector pushed Bitsy into the room as both policemen drew their guns.

The footsteps continued to the stairs, down the steps, into the hall at the bottom, periodically pausing as if stopping at each room's entrance, checking inside. The older policeman flattened himself unseen at the right side of the door, his handgun aimed at the entrance. The tall one positioned himself at the other side, pushing Bitsy behind him. Shielded by his back, she sensed his trained tautness. Her own muscles clutched with terror. The footsteps had stopped at the room next door. They started again, slow, hesitant. The policeman's shoulders and spine were rigid, his body ready. Bitsy held her breath.

Gwen appeared in the doorway, tiny in the tall jamb. She gasped, her hand flying to the hollow of her throat. "Bitsy?"

Relief seemed to melt Bitsy's very marrow. She started to step out from behind Hector. "Gwen, thank goodness, it's—"

Hector pulled her roughly back behind him.

"Hey, let go!" She tried to shake his hand off her arm.

Hector's partner stepped out from the wall. Gwen, her features frozen with fear, looked from one pointed gun to the other.

"Bitsy?" Her voice was thin, wavering. "What's going on?"

Bitsy tried to sidestep Hector once more, but his grip only tightened on her forearm.

"At ease, big boy," she snapped at him. "Put your gun back where it belongs," she ordered the other cop. "Can't you see the poor child is terrified?"

"What's your name?" Hector barked.

Gwen stared at the gun pointed at her heart. Her throat worked but no sound came out.

"Gwen Rinkert," Bitsy supplied. "She works here."

The policemen didn't lower their weapons.

"Go ahead," Bitsy encouraged. "Tell them all about the 'corpse' that came in earlier today."

Gwen looked from the gun to Bitsy to the police. Trying to avoid looking at the aimed guns, she said, "I came on about nine tonight. The corpse was already here."

"Was it dead?" Hector demanded.

Gwen's incredulousness momentarily eclipsed her fear. "Officers, with all due respect, that is the definition of a corpse."

"He wasn't dead," Bitsy contradicted. "Less than twenty minutes ago, he sat up right here." She pointed at the gurney. "And said, 'Something tells me this isn't the Pearly Gates.' He was blond, blue-eyed, tall. I'd say six-two, like the report. He was well built. He obviously worked out." She stared at the empty metal bed. "He had a good smile."

"He couldn't have gotten too far," Hector said to his partner. "Get on the radio and see if there's immediate backup in the area. Call the station and tell them we're going to need more men. He could be to the border by the time we get done checking every masked person out there."

By the time Hector had ushered the women upstairs, Bitsy heard the wail of an approaching siren. When the other cop came back from the squad car, Hector pointed at Gwen and said, "I'll stay here with her until back-up arrives." His finger swung to Bitsy. "You take her downtown for further questioning."

"What for?" Bitsy demanded as the older cop grasped her upper arm. "Am I being charged with something?"

"We just want to ask you a few more questions," the older cop reassured her, steering her toward the front door.

Bitsy glanced over her shoulder as she was ushered out the door. She called to Gwen, "Get ahold of Grey."

The cop opened the car's door and she slid into the back of the cruiser with its unique odor of heavy, desperate sweats.

Costumed children came around the far corner, headed to the first house at the end of the street. In the split second before the car door slammed closed, Bitsy heard the night's calling card.

"Trick or treat."

Chapter Two

"An APB, Arthur?" Mick asked. His last identity had been Michael James, but he had quickly become known as Mick and preferred it. Only Arthur insisted on the more formal name he'd last christened the man.

Arthur opened the white van's side panel. The metallic sign on the driver's door said Frieda's House of Flora and Fauna. Arthur was a spare man, elegant in body and movement. Forbearance in his stance and natural expression, he stood by the openmouthed van and waited.

Mick's gaze shifted from the black insides of the van to the tempered features of his mentor. "I need an explanation."

"An explanation?" The older man employed the same economy of speech as he did in physical appearance.

"I wake up, not at the arranged location with instructions for my next assignment, but—" he gestured at the building behind them "—at a funeral fun house greeted by the beautiful Bitsy of the mortuary business and her glad bag of embalming tools."

"Bitsy." Arthur tested the name.

"You descend from Mount Olympus or whatever lofty peak Central occupies these days, complete with a chariot. Not to mention, thanks to San Francisco's boys in blue, my identity has been compromised up and down the California coast."

A siren wailed through the night.

Arthur looked at Mick. He smiled pleasantly. "Shall we go?"

"What's going on, Arthur?"

The other man had rounded the front of the van and was climbing into the driver's seat. He buckled and adjusted his seat belt, smoothed his pants' creases and started the engine. He turned in the seat, and with genteel features and a civil smile, he looked at Mick. "Get in, Michael."

Something was very wrong.

Mick climbed inside the back of the van, slamming the side door shut behind him. The van was dark, no overhead light, no seats in the back. Arthur waited until Mick arranged himself on the cool metal floor, then eased the van out from behind the funeral home's storage shed.

Mick's questions started immediately. "Did last night's operation go down as planned?"

"Shh." Arthur raised a tapered finger. "Let me have my Mel Gibson getaway moment here."

Mick shook his head, a smile starting as the van

smoothly accelerated to thirty miles per hour and held steady. "Yeah, you're one big bad ass, Arthur."

"Yes," was all the other man would concede.

They drove in silence, away from the sirens. It was futile to ask any more questions. Arthur would give him the answers when he was ready. Mick saw Arthur touch the pearl-gray streak at his temple. Beneath that rakish silver wave, there was a scar. Beneath that a metal plate.

"Congressman Kittredge was shot this evening," Arthur said.

Mick listened and waited. The old man had never uttered an unnecessary word in his life.

"He was leaving a late dinner at a Bay Area restaurant when a man wearing a Halloween mask approached. The valet saw the gun and pushed Kittredge out of the way. The bullet hit the congressman's shoulder instead of his heart. The valet's a hero. The assassin got away."

The sheet was loosening about Mick's body. He pulled it tighter. He could feel the texture of the road through the van's bare floor.

"They're going to say you did it," Arthur told him.

Mick closed his eyes. There was a rolling, soothing movement to the blackness.

"I issued the APB, tipped off the locals about the location of the funeral home."

Mick's eyes opened.

"If the local police had found you sooner, it could've provided an alibi. At the very least, protection. Until I could get to you, you were safer in the company of the police than our own men." The old man's hands were steady on the wheel, his gaze aimed straight into the night.

"I didn't mean to involve the woman. Bitsy."

The name sounded across the empty van. Mick saw the woman in stilettos stomping around the room, brandishing a scalpel, spouting indignation.

"She's an alibi for you. A liability for the Agency."

Mick's hand fisted, ached to slam against the floor. He resisted. The gesture was ineffectual. Unvented rage was not.

"I erased your identity," Arthur continued.

"If the Agency is trying to get me killed, they won't be too happy about that."

"It's to protect the Agency as much as you. When the feds or the locals look, they'll find nothing, a man who never existed. Still they'll have your name. Others will know it. Grainy photos, a crude sketch or two will follow. It's out of my control now, Michael."

Mick waited for Arthur to tell him more, to give him a rationale. The darkness and the silence became too much, so finally he asked, "Why?"

The other man's eyes looked into the night. "There's not always an explanation, Michael. Life is random. Hit or miss. You stepped into its path."

"What about the raid on the arms smugglers last night?"

"They got seven arrests, little fish, some AK-47s."

Arthur's voice was flat. "The operation was compromised. There was a leak. The key figures had got out of the U.S. and escaped back to the Far East by last night."

Mick's fingers remained furled into a tight ball. Since the first death, he'd held fast to his rage. "The operation was deliberately sabotaged." His voice was as level as his mentor's.

"An investigation on the incident will be conducted through the traditional channels," Arthur said.

"It should've gone down as planned."

"Life," Arthur said. "Hit or miss." He touched his temple.

Mick knew he wouldn't get much more information. The Agency's M.O. was maximum secrecy equated maximum security and efficiency. Agents reported to an assigned contact. They were given only the necessary information to carry out their assignments. Each agent knew if their cover was blown, they'd be abandoned. It was the sacrifice of one for the survival of many. If nothing went wrong, the system worked.

Something had gone wrong.

Mick looked at the man driving, the man who'd engineered his first death, and in doing so, had saved his life. Since that time, he'd died a hundred deaths, a hundred different ways, none of them real, all of them resulting in greater good…until now.

Mick looked at the man he loved. "Who ordered my setup?"

Quiet was the only answer. Mick's words hovered in the silence.

"Kittredge, our own agents, an international arms ring... It's someone big, isn't it?" Mick said.

Arthur's gaze stayed on the road. "Rot starts at the top."

"Corbain." Mick muttered the name of the outsider put in charge of the Agency after last year's presidential election.

Arthur steered the van into the parking lot of a convenience store. The lot was empty except for a car parked to the far side and a pickup truck near the entrance. He pulled up to the pumps and turned off the engine.

"I've brought you as far as I can. I'll fill the tank. There's a change of clothes in the bag back there. Money, identification, a name and number on a card in the glove compartment. Friends of mine. They own a twenty-two-foot whaler that can get you across the Gulf."

Mick looked at his oldest friend. "You didn't have to do this. If they find out..."

Arthur looked at him for a moment, then said the words he'd said to Mick twelve years ago. "Everybody deserves a chance." He opened the door.

"Arthur?" Mick placed his hand on the other man's forearm. "Thank you."

When the older man's gaze met his own, Mick could almost read his thoughts. Arthur had had to make a choice once before. He feared he had chosen wrong.

"You'll be on your own now," Arthur said. "Stay alive."

The driver's door closed. Mick waited but didn't hear the gas cap being unscrewed or the gurgle of gas into the tank. Rising to his knees behind the front seat, he saw large signs on the pumps instructing customers to pay inside before pumping. Arthur was walking toward the store. Only the streaks of gray at either temple revealed the years that had passed since he'd recruited Mick. Even then, the poreless skin had been fine-lined, the slants deep from nose to mouth.

Mick reached into the bag of clothes when he felt an unwelcome pressure against his bladder. He looked around the lot. There was a bathroom at the end of the building.

Mick scanned the lot once more. Inside the store, he could see Arthur standing before one of the candy bar displays. A man, mid-twenties, came out of the store, got in the pickup and drove off. Mick grabbed a pair of sweatpants, slipped on the running shoes, slid open the van door and, gathering the sheet tighter, stepped out.

The bathroom door was locked.

Behind the store, darkness almost hid a stand of trees. He headed toward them.

He moved behind a thick trunk, back far enough so he could see the lot, but no one could see him. A dark Chevy turned into the lot. It pulled up to the pumps, opposite the van, and parked.

Arthur had come out of the store and was walking toward the vehicle, a chocolate bar in his hand. He unwrapped the candy, broke off a square, put it into his mouth.

Mick finished and was pulling up the too-short sweatpants that ended several inches above his ankles. He scanned the lot. It was quiet. No one had gotten out of the dark sedan. Mick's instinct of twelve years undercover awoke. His mouth was forming the word No as the sedan's window lowered and a fat steel cylinder appeared. A muted *pop-pop-pop*... Arthur dropping. Several more pops and the sedan sped away, gone as if it'd never been.

Mick was running now. He reached Arthur and dragged his body away from the pumps. The clerk looked out the wide front windows.

"Call an ambulance," Mick yelled. He looked down at the man in his arms. He'd been hit once in the heart, twice in the forehead. Execution-style.

Mick looked to the pumps, the van, saw the dark stream where shots had punctured the side of the vehicle, the half-empty gas tank with its lethal fumes. He felt the intuitive quiver, the anticipation of disaster, his muscles tightening. "Get out," he yelled to the clerk coming out the door. "Get out of here!"

He covered Arthur's body with his own. At first, the explosion was contained, almost anticlimactic. Then, the fuel tank ignited. Light flashed and noon changed places with the night. Mick felt the wave of heat roll over his body. He looked up. The clerk was running to his car parked at the far end of the lot. Mick rolled off Arthur and dragged him toward the woods.

Beneath the long shadows of the trees, Mick placed his mouth on Arthur's and he breathed into the man, even knowing it was as useless as a fist slamming against metal. The sweet smell of chocolate met him. He checked Arthur's neck, then the wrist above the hand that still clutched the half-wrapped Cadbury bar.

Mick looked back toward the van. A spark shot up, and in a blast of color and light, the gas pumps blew. The heat reached for the men. The California sky was fragmented, fluorescent.

The sedan had headed south, back toward Canaan. Mick stared into the heat and light. Cars from the highway were slowing down, stopping. Emergency vehicles would be here soon.

He worked quickly, drawing back Arthur's linen sport coat, unfastening the holster that held the 9 mm, retrieved a leather wallet from the coat's inside pocket. The wallet held only a few singles, a fake driver's license and an American Express gold card in the same false name. Either item would only alert Mick's enemies should he try to use them. He took out the singles, slipped them into the sweatpants' pocket and shoved the wallet back into the jacket's inside pocket.

A new siren pierced the night. Close by. Mick pulled up Arthur's carefully creased right trouser leg, released the gun strapped to the ankle and wrapped it high on his own calf so the short sweat-pants would conceal it. He straightened the trouser, smoothed the coat, aligning the gold buttons. The sirens sounded closer, were almost here.

He straightened the angle of Arthur's head, folded his beautifully shaped hands into a position of peace across his chest. He leaned over, kissed the man, rose and walked into the night.

DAWN HAD BROKEN, spreading a surreal cast across the night sky as Grey Torre drove Bitsy back to Memorial Manor. His black Lexus pulled up smoothly beside Bitsy's car, contrasting with the bright apple-green hatchback, a color everyone, including Bitsy, found nauseous, but had gotten Bitsy a great deal on the car.

"Thank you again for coming down to the station," she told Grey.

"Damsels in distress are my specialty." Grey gave her the infamous grin that had charmed females from the corner kiosk to the higher courts. Bitsy had known that irresistible smile since she used to challenge Grey two Scooter Pies she could climb to the top of ol' lady Simone's sycamore before he could. She'd won every time.

"I was only drinking a Corona, watching CNN," Grey assured her. "Some nut tried to kill Congress-man Kittredge last night. Damn crazies. One of my old buddies from Berkeley, Tim Stafford, works for Kittredge. Says he's the real ticket—a politician who actually cares about his constituents."

Grey looked pointedly at her. "The moral is 'you can never be too careful.' I'm thinking of having that tattooed on your beautiful backside."

"Leave my beautiful backside out of this," she warned him. "I don't go around advertising for big bad bogeymen to come and take advantage of me."

"And still, they seem to find you no matter how hard you hide."

"I'm not hiding," she insisted as she opened the car door. "I'm just…" Her words faltered as she turned to her friend. "I'm just…"

Grey's voice softened. "I know, honey, I know. C'mon, I'll walk you to your car."

"Really I'm doing fine, Grey," Bitsy assured him. He had draped his arm across her shoulders as they headed to her car, and she patted his hand and felt the pull of weariness.

"It's your heart," Grey decided. "It's too big. It keeps getting stepped on."

She yearned to lean on the welcome weight of her friend. While the puff of her pompadour had long surrendered, and she had a run in the left leg of her hose, Grey looked, as always, as if he'd just stepped from the pages of *InStyle*.

She straightened. A few hours sleep and her physical exhaustion would be remedied. Her shattered illusion of safety, however, wouldn't be so easily restored. The man in the embalming room had dredged up old feelings, fears, everything she'd worked so hard to keep under control the last few months.

"The bum was probably past the county line before they even called for backup," Grey said.

"Thanks to me."

"It was an honest mistake, Bits. The fact is, more creeps than we want to consider get away without paying for their crimes. Look at your ex-husband."

Grey had handled her divorce. He was one of California's most successful divorce lawyers, his skill at securing his female clients generous settlements earning him the nickname the Spago Ladies' Lawyer. Bitsy's divorce hadn't earned him his usual fabulous fees since she had wanted none of the Dumont fortune. Grey had also done his best to keep the entire affair out of the press, although most big-time divorce lawyers would have taken the case for the publicity alone. Even still, Jumpin' Johnny Dumont, known for his lavish lifestyle and bad-boy antics, was a media favorite, and his divorce from his small-town Cinderella had made as good cover as when he'd married her eighteen months earlier in a whirl-wind romance.

"They don't put you behind bars for breaking hearts, Grey."

He said nothing. He had mentioned the bruises only once. She had asked him never to mention them again.

"Come on." Grey made his voice light. "I'll buy you a tofu omelet."

She made a face. "Bean curd isn't my idea of comfort food." She stopped a few steps from her car, turned and faced him. "Besides, I'm beat."

"All right, I'll accept that, but only because I've got some tax records to go over before I drive down to meet a client this morning."

"Beverly Hills?" she guessed.

"Malibu," Grey answered with a toothy smile. "I'm driving up to the lodge next weekend. You come, too. Try a little rock climbing."

"Rock climbing?" She shook her head. "I like to keep my feet on the ground nowadays."

Grey looked down at her. "That's not my 'two Scooter Pies' Bitsy talking."

She looked up at her friend. "No, it's not." Tiredness was tangible in her words.

"I'm calling you next week, and you better be ready to scale some peaks."

She was too exhausted even to try to think of an excuse. She touched Grey's arm. "Thank you again for coming."

"No problem. It'll give me an amusing story to tell in chambers." He leaned down and gave her a light kiss on her forehead. "Go home. Get some sleep. Wash off that makeup. I keep waiting for you to say, 'I'm ready for my close-up, Mr. DeMille.'"

She smiled. "I love you, Grey."

Grey straightened and regarded her with a similar smile. "Don't think that's going to scare me away. You know I don't give up easily."

"I've got the cavities to prove it."

She went to her car, unlocked the door and slid into the driver's seat. Through the side window, she watched Grey walk back to his car, turning his collar up against the early morning chill coming in from the coast. She started the engine and waved goodbye as he reached his own car. He was a good man. A lousy tree climber, but a good man.

She pulled out of the parking lot and headed toward home, trying not to think about last night, trying not to think at all. The day's light had erased the night, but, in her mind's eye, she still saw the man with the slow smile and the eyes of a storm.

She'd been so careful this time. She'd arranged her life neatly, forced herself to stop and look before leaping. Truth be told, her current vampire vixen getup was the wildest thing she had allowed herself since her divorce. And considering it had been Halloween in Canaan, she had still been among the conservative faction of the town's population.

For months, she had bitten her tongue, ignored desires, walked calmly away instead of rushing headfirst into the flames. It hadn't mattered. Michael James had made her realize what she'd feared deep down all along was true. She was not safe.

She shook her head to clear the man's image from her mind, releasing a sigh of relief at her close call. The man was a criminal, for goodness sake, reaffirming her belief she couldn't trust her own faculties of attraction. Desire clouded the mind, sent logic and common sense scurrying.

She took a deep breath, hands steady on the wheel, and moved the car forward at a reasonable speed. Her composed world had been threatened, but it wouldn't be toppled by one smiling stiff. Last night was already on its way to becoming an anecdote for Grey's colleagues. According to the police, Michael James was probably heading to the border. And she was on her way home to take a long, hot shower, crawl into bed with the latest Mary Higgins Clark novel and dismiss the brief, disturbing appearance of Michael James in her life.

She reached for the radio's buttons, the quiet she usually sought seeming unnaturally still. As she clicked the radio's on button, she heard a voice, but it did not come from the speakers. It came from directly behind her. A voice she'd heard before. A voice she'd never expected to hear again.

"Beautiful day to be alive, isn't it, darling?" Michael James observed from the car's backseat.

Chapter Three

The hell with control. Bitsy screamed so loud the windows vibrated.

In the rearview mirror, the man winced. "Is that necessary?"

She screamed again, louder and longer.

The man rubbed the back of his neck. "That's not really helping matters."

She slammed on the brakes and grabbed the door handle. At the same time, the man's broad hand snaked from behind the seat and snapped down the lock button.

"I'm not going to hurt you."

She twisted her head, meeting the man's eyes.

"I'm one of the good guys," he said. His lips parted in a thin smile, the mouth sensual with a touch of cruelness.

Her fear intensified. "Not according to your APB."

His smile faded, leaving his features gray and drawn. "Just drive," he ordered.

She faced front. Her hands gripped the steering wheel as if it were a life preserver. He was scared, too, she realized. A tiny bit of her fear slipped away, making room for rational thought. After her marriage, she had bought a weight bench and a set of weights, and lifted every other day. She'd taken self-defense seminars and had gotten up to a green belt in tae kwon do until a torn hamstring had set her back. She had promised herself she would never be a victim again.

She would keep that promise.

She looked through the windshield, hopeful for any sign of life in this small square of the City of Death. All was quiet.

"Where do you want to go?" She asked. *Better*, she thought. Controlled. Calm. She had to stay cool. If she gave in to the panic coursing through her, the man would win. And she could lose her life.

She glanced in the rearview mirror, saw his gaze nonchalantly lift to hers. She could taste her fear. Like bile, it rose in her throat. She looked away. Damn him.

He leaned in close behind her until she could see the sharply drawn lines of his features in her peripheral vision. His fingers rested on the side of the seat right near her shoulder. One inch closer and those at-ease fingers could wrap about her throat; those nails with their pale half moons could line up like little soldiers along her jugular.

"To your house," he whispered. A bolt of ice darted up her spine.

The man sat back, the pressure along her seat relenting. Still, his hand remained, deceptively lifeless, on the side of the seat. She slid her foot off the brake to the gas pedal. She released the clutch, not realizing the car was still in third gear. The engine seized. The car bucked. The man swore as he was thrown into the back of her seat. Bitsy was slammed into the steering wheel. She straightened, her hands clutching the wheel as if in spasm.

"Okay, I'm going to give you the benefit of the doubt on that one. Never did meet a woman who could handle a stick."

She wrapped her hand around the black knob of the shifter, its hardness beneath her palm. No give, no take. She shifted into first, eased up on the clutch and gently pressed down on the gas. The car moved forward as smoothly as hot fudge melting on French vanilla ice cream. *Control.*

The street was empty. People were sleeping. Dream now, she told them, as the car passed house after silent house. Dream sweet, illicit dreams.

The police station was in the opposite direction the car had been heading. If she could keep the man preoccupied while taking a series of lefts and rights, he might not notice they were turning around.

"How'd you avoid the police?" she asked. She sounded good. Efficient, in charge.

When he didn't answer her, she glanced up to the mirror and saw his fingers rake through his hair, a gesture that was becoming too familiar.

"There was an APB issued—" she began again.

The man leaned forward. Bitsy stiffened.

"That was a mistake."

The breath of his words moved past her. She knew he'd seen her body tense.

"That's what every criminal says."

"Criminal?"

She couldn't believe the man actually sounded disgusted. "You're a wanted man."

"I'm the good guy." She heard the bitterness in his tone.

As she slowed the car to turn left, she glanced in the rearview mirror. The man had taken the sheet from the funeral home, wrapped it around his waist and slung one end over his shoulder toga-style. Only now he had pants on, at least.

"You slipped out, put the sheet over your head and joined last night's Halloween festivities?" she guessed, trying to keep his attention.

The man was looking out the window. "Nah, I crawled into a casket. Took a little nap."

She glanced up and saw the man's easy grin. Not exactly her idea of a cold-blooded criminal. Then again, her character antennae had been whacked out since her first adolescent hormonal rush.

She took another left. "So, if you're the good guy, Mr. James, why are you being chased by the SFPD?"

"Call me Mick."

"Okay, what'd you do to upset San Francisco's finest, not to mention our local boys in blue, Mick?" She bit down on the hard *K*. "Nothing?"

His eyes, as unclouded as a child's, met hers in the mirror. "I'm in danger."

Bitsy steered right, looking away from those eyes. Eyes lied as easily as lips.

"And so are you."

Bitsy looked in the mirror before making another turn. "That's pretty obvious to me, Mick." Again, the cutting *K*.

His eyes were steady and dark blue in the reflection. "I was set up. Soon I'll be charged with a crime I didn't commit. Except I've got an alibi—you. So now, when they learn I'm not dead, they don't only have to find me and kill me. They have to kill you, too. And this time the deaths will be real."

"For an innocent man, you certainly seem to attract your share of enemies, Mick. First, the police. Now, murderers."

"One man is dead already. Another was almost killed last night."

"And you're innocent."

"I don't know any man who's innocent," her captor said. "But I didn't do the crimes they'll say I did."

Bitsy knew those blue eyes were looking at her in the mirror, asking her to believe him. She kept her gaze on the road.

Behind her, Mick swore. He'd seen the parked black-and-white sedan with the row of red lights across the roof the same time she had.

She checked the mirror. She didn't see Mick.

Instead she heard, "Don't do anything stupid. I'll use this if I have to."

A hard point jabbed her through the back of her seat. He had a gun. She couldn't speak, she couldn't breathe. All her control dissolved. Her life was reduced to a half-inch circle at the base of her spine.

He jabbed her again, low at her back, and she felt fear flow from that point right up her backbone. Adrenaline overwhelmed her brain, her body. Everything seemed to speed up, yet slow down at the same time.

"You better pray they didn't see me," she heard him threaten.

She'd dealt with death every day, foolishly thinking she'd forged a pact with its unreasonableness. But here it was, the ultimate master of ceremonies. *Let me live*, she prayed.

She glanced in the mirror, not expecting to see the man. But could he see her if she tried to signal the police? Taking a chance right now could be deadly. So was not taking one.

"Keep your gaze straight ahead," Mick ordered. "Don't even think of looking to the right."

The gun bore into her back. She pulled even with the police cruiser, then past it. The chance was gone.

"Are we close to your house?" he asked.

"Yes." The word came out anguished.

"For your sake, I hope so."

She arched her lower back, moving her slim vertebrae away from the focused pressure on her back. In her mind, she could see the hole formed by a bullet, a perfect polka dot piercing her skin, her spine, her organs. Her terror fed on itself now, widening, overtaking her.

She forced herself to concentrate.

She couldn't risk going to the police station. Maybe if she got him inside her house, she could find a weapon or call the police. "Won't be but a minute," she assured the man, her voice June Cleaver surreal.

The man said nothing.

Did he have a full clip in his gun, she wondered. She slowed down and took a right, then another and another until the car was turned around again, heading back to her house. In mute panic, she watched the police car grow smaller until it disappeared from the mirror.

"Are we almost there?" the man asked after a few silent minutes.

"Yes," Bitsy replied. There was a warm, metallic sensation in her mouth. She'd bitten into her own lip and drawn blood.

The man stayed down, said nothing. She heard his even breathing, his steady, too quiet threat. She smelled the lingering chemical odor from the embalming room. The fluid of death. Her stomach roiled. She feared she'd get sick. She felt the touch of death at her backbone and prayed desperately for another day.

They pulled into the driveway of the stucco bungalow she rented in a quiet neighborhood of similar stucco and clapboard bungalows. She saw the delicate scalloped line of the eaves. She saw the tangle of rosebushes along the trellised front porch. They'd been pruned, in preparation for winter. Still, several thorny trailers continued to grow. She stared at those stubborn tentacles of new green. Tears filled her eyes. *Control.* The word came like a mantra. *Control, Bitsy.*

She pushed the garage-door opener on the visor, waited while the door rose, steered inside. She turned off the car's engine, but clung to the steering wheel to keep her hands from shaking. Still the tremors seized her, and her body trembled.

"We're here," she said, sounding like the gracious hostage.

"Shut the garage door."

She did as he said. The door dropped, sealing her farther off from salvation. After its final rattle, she saw the shock of blond hair first, rising cautiously. His eyes, alert, canvassed the inside of the garage, the side door. The pressure against her back stayed. "This is where you live?"

Bitsy nodded.

"Alone?"

She nodded again.

"Any animals? A dog? A cat?"

She shook her head.

"If we step inside and I find out otherwise, I'll kill them."

"There's only me."

"All right. Let's go."

She got out of the car and he was immediately right behind her, gripping her upper arm. She tried to step and her knees buckled. He caught her. The dull point of the gun, covered by the sheet folded across his arm, pressed into her ribs. The heat of his body mixed with the heat of her fear.

"You should get a pet," he suggested as they headed with awkward steps to the side door. "A little dog or a cat, maybe."

At the door, he bent over and picked up the keys that had fallen from her shaking hands. "It's not good to live all alone." He inserted the key into the door, but before he turned it, the door swung open.

He looked down at Bitsy.

"I must've left it unlocked last night," she said. "I was in a hurry."

He twisted the key out, watching her. "You should be more careful," he advised, then pushed her inside.

As soon as he released her, Bitsy took several steps into the house, but her progress was stopped abruptly.

"Bravo, Bitsy," a woman's voice said. "You finally brought home a live one."

Lanie stepped into the kitchen. She wore a pair of Bitsy's shorts, a T-shirt and a pair of turquoise flip-flops with plastic butterflies along their straps. A tall black witch's hat sat on the kitchen table atop the heaped remains of the rest of the costume. The woman's well-placed features resembled Bitsy's, except, as she crossed her arms and leaned against the refrigerator, Lanie's held the wry amusement of an older cousin who'd always enjoyed the advantage of power by birth date alone.

"Lanie," Bitsy warned.

As the name left her mouth, Mick grasped her wrist and pulled her tightly against him in a false embrace. At her hip bone, his other hand pressed the gun into her belly. She instinctively recoiled. He released her wrist to wrap his arm around her neck, pressing her mouth closer to his.

"Don't," he whispered like a deadly kiss.

She felt the length of cool steel, its hard edge against the yield of flesh. The heat of her blood rose. The pulse in her throat beneath his palm quickened. All reasoning left her. Only instinct allowed her to speak in a breathless tone to her cousin.

"What are you doing here, Lanie?"

"I had a fight with Roy last night. Just because he was dressed as Casper the Friendly Ghost didn't mean he could spend half the night in a corner with a Wonder Woman wannabe. So, I crashed here. How come you didn't show up? Oops, dumb question. I can see—"

"Lanie?" Bitsy's voice sounded more strangled than passionate.

"Yes, right." Lanie misinterpreted the urgency in her cousin's voice. "I can see you're occupied, so I'll just discreetly let myself out."

Lanie gathered her costume, plopping the witch's hat on her head. As she passed them, she tugged on the sheet wrapped around Mick's middle. "It seems my cousin and I share the same fondness for friendly ghosts."

She gave Mick a wink, flashed a smile at Bitsy and was gone. The side door banged, then all was quiet. Bitsy was once again alone with a madman.

Chapter Four

"She doesn't live here," Bitsy blurted. "I had no idea she'd be here."

They stood, breast to chest, thigh to thigh, belly to belly, only a metal snout and a chamber of bullets between them. Bitsy found Mick's eyes, hot and bright.

"She's gone. Let me go."

"I didn't hear a car leave."

"She lives four blocks over, three houses down."

Mick muttered an obscenity, his breath warm and unwashed on her. She held his gaze, her thoughts the same as his. Lanie strolls home, slips the waiting *Canaan Courier* out of the mailbox or snaps on the 6:00 a.m. news, and sees a picture of her little cousin's one-night stand splashed across the front page or flashed on the screen. He shouldn't have let her go. He made a mistake. A sly satisfaction spread though Bitsy's veins.

Mick's jaw set. "Where's a phone?"

She tipped her head to the left, where a cordless

phone on its charger sat on the small table against the wall.

"Get it." He released her. The relief drove her backward and made her light-headed. The gun stayed trained on her abdomen. The light-headed moment passed. She took two more steps backward and picked up the phone.

He reached for it, clasped it in one hand and punched in the number, his gaze aimed at her.

"It's me," he said to whoever picked up at the other end. A pause followed as he listened. His lips close to the mouthpiece, he then said, "He's dead. Only one death reported." Another pause, the silence laden.

"No, don't come in. Too much risk. Too many involved." His gaze was as steady on her as the gun. "I'll meet you. I have resources. Find out what you can. I'll call." He paused. "Only as a last resort." Another beat, then he said, "I have a guest." A metallic tone had infused his voice. No expression lit his hard face. Bitsy stared at the dull silver gun, stifling an impulse to let her knees buckle.

"I'll be in touch." He disconnected and handed Bitsy the phone.

"Who's dead?" she asked, surprised at her voice's remote quality.

"We need clothes, any cash, food." He ignored her question. "An ATM card, a cell phone and charger." He ticked the items off as if they were on their way to a weekend in the wine country.

When she didn't move, he reached for her arm. She recoiled and stood strong. Mick's gaze snapped to hers. It was a matter of wills now, even as the piercing fear deep and unspeakable, welled up, pushing at her limits and she grieved for her lost courage.

"If I was going to kill you, I would have by now." He sounded weary. Neither of them had slept.

She regarded him in the yellow, florid light. He was a mystery, a danger, yet he made her want to believe in him. Her anger at this parlor trick was like a keen rising in her head and much more valuable than her fear.

"We have to go now, or we won't have a chance." He continued the ruse. Her anger was to the point of blaring.

"I'm not the one wanted by the police, Mick." His name sounded hard on her tongue.

His smile wasn't warm. "No, the people who want you are much more dangerous."

"Only one man is holding a gun on me now."

His lips pulled back farther from his teeth in a devil's grin. "Right now you're lucky." He glanced at the wall clock. Bitsy estimated her cousin should be cutting though McGilicuddy's backyard with its plastercraft planters and ceramic gnomes. Mick gestured with the gun toward the entryway into the rest of the house. "Clothes, cash, food," he said as if ordering from a Chinese menu.

Her gut turning, Bitsy backed out of the room, feeling it fatal not to face him. Under the weight of his eyes, she moved, startled when she hit the doorjamb, then she was in the hall, the tidy living room with its coordinated furniture and the Roman shades she'd bought on end-of-the-season clearance from Sears.

"Clothes, Mick?" Her lips thinned and her voice mocked. "Unless you're a misses size six, you're SOL."

He didn't look worried and that made her wonder. "The clothes are for you." His heavy gaze dropped, then sidled back up her until her skin prickled.

"You're afraid I'll look conspicuous?" She returned the same once-over. "And you won't?"

He moved toward her as she spoke, forcing her farther down the hall, a frantic pitch of resistance and disbelief vibrating inside her.

"Do I look like a worried man, Bitsy?" His voice softened, designed to throw her off balance more than a sharp pitch.

They were almost to her bedroom with its slightly sleazy black-lacquered furniture and oversize Georgia O'Keeffe framed floral prints. The bathroom was to their left. Bitsy stopped.

"What?" Impatience cracked Mick's voice.

She screwed up her forehead, her eyes becoming larger, the pupils contracted. "I have to go."

His features showed no sign of his impatience easing. Her fear and anger remained near at hand. Her resolve strengthened. She shrugged, took a step toward the bathroom door as if she didn't need his permission.

His hand snapped around her wrist.

"What?" She twisted her arm but he held firm. "I can't go to the bathroom?"

With the gun, he pushed back the half-opened door and pulled her into the bathroom with him. He scanned the room, the small narrow window with its lowered vinyl mini-blinds, the teal-and-peach ceramic tile halfway up the walls, the shower curtain with pink flamingos stretched across the tub.

"Okay." He thrust her toward the toilet as he let go of her wrist.

"Okay?" she blurted. "What do you expect me to do? Go at gunpoint?"

He stepped past her, pushed up the blinds and checked the window's lock. Bitsy glanced in the mirror over the sink, gave a sharp intake of breath.

"What?" Mick wheeled from the secured window.

Bitsy peered at her reflection, the sunken eyes, the skin gray with fatigue and stress beneath the garish remains of her makeup. "I knew you looked like crap, but I didn't think I looked this bad." She pushed a lank lock of hair off her brow.

Mick stepped back. "You've got one minute. I'll be right outside."

He rounded the door, pulling it half-closed behind him. She waited for it to close totally.

It didn't.

"You're not going to close the door?"

"Fifty seconds." His shoulder and arm, the gun dangling in his hand, were visible at the door's edge.

"What do you think I'm going to do?" She pulled down her stockings, panties. "Hang myself from the shower?"

"Forty-five seconds."

"Pull out the .44 I keep in the back of the toilet tank?"

"Thirty-five seconds."

"You're not making this any easier." She rattled the toilet paper holder, ripped off a length.

"Thirty seconds."

She flushed, pulled up her panties, adjusted her stockings, twisted the hot and cold water faucets all the way open.

"Ten seconds."

"I'm washing my hands," she yelled back.

"Five, four…"

The water stopped. "I'm drying my hands."

"Three, two…" The door started to swing open.

"One," Bitsy yelled, aimed the value-size can of extra-hold hair spray at Mick's face and sprayed full force into his surprised blue eyes. She heard a guttural gurgle as she pushed past him. His hands reached for her but, blinded, he only found a fistful of the hairpiece she'd added to last night's costume. She jerked her head hard as he yanked the opposite way, and the hairpiece ripped loose. She ran. She was down the hall, into the kitchen when he came behind her, spewing passionate oaths aimed at her and her children and her children's children. She heard him hit something hard and curse loudly. She looked frantically for her car keys but didn't see them on the table or counters. She was running out of time. Undoing the lock on the side door, she dashed out, slamming the door behind her. *Freedom* was her wildly delicious, delirious last thought…till she ran head-on into a mountainous, unmoving mass. She bounced back onto the concrete floor and was knocked out cold.

SHE WAS BEING HOISTED UP under the armpits when she came to. In front of her in her garage stood an angular man with a thin face and hatchet features, pointing a gun casually at the left side of her chest where her heart pounded crazily. Twice in one day. Go figure.

Bitsy jumped as someone behind her wrenched her arms together and bound her wrists with a hard tie that sliced into her skin. She whipped her head around and found the no-necked brick wall that had stopped her escape. She twisted her head farther and saw the razor-thin wire circling her wrists. Any attempts to escape its hold would only result in slicing through flesh, arteries, veins.

She turned back to the front. Her gaze careened around the garage. She saw nothing of the blue-eyed, charming-smile son of a bitch who'd gotten her into this mess in the first place.

Was Mick dead? The thought hit her harder than the mass of muscle behind her. Had the man with the cold fish eyes in front of her killed him with the gun now holding her hostage?

"Let's go." The man gestured with the gun.

Holding her bound wrists, the gorilla nudged her forward. *Control,* Bitsy repeated to herself as she was led to a gray BMW. *Stay in control.* She frantically searched for self-defense techniques. *Look for an advantage.* The creep behind her was so close, she could feel his erection pressing into her. Her wrists were bound behind her back, but her feet were free.

The thug gripping her arms released one to open the car door. As he pushed her in, she aimed her spiked heels at his groin and got off a couple good shots to his shins. He let out a yelp as he shoved her down into the backseat.

"You wanna play rough?" He came at her, his shaved head ducking her flailing feet. His hand came up, struck her hard once, twice. Her head whipped right and left. Her brain rattled.

"Cut out the social niceties," the other man growled as he slid into the driver's seat. "There'll be plenty of time for that later." He looked over his shoulder and gave Bitsy a sickly grin that soured her stomach.

The strong arms shoved Bitsy back into the seat, grabbed her ankles with one hand and circled them with the thin wire. She gingerly prodded with her tongue several teeth loosened by the blows.

"There, honey." The ape leaned over her, his thick lips rolled back from his pale-pink gums. The moist smell of male sweat and cigarettes overwhelmed her. "This is only the beginning. Whatever god you believe in, I'll have you screaming for him before I'm done with you."

She screwed up her lips and spat at him. Blood colored the saliva that dripped down his cheek.

The fist that hit her square in the face and knocked her out cold again was almost a relief.

When she came to, she was uncertain how much time had passed, but didn't think much. The blood was still damp on her skin, the pain fresh where the fist had met her face. The ache in her shoulders had not yet escalated from a throb, but her wrists and ankles burned where the wire cut into the thin skin.

She kept her eyes closed, hoping the cover of unconsciousness would give her captors a false sense of security, perhaps cause them to talk more freely, reveal something useful. Something that could save her.

The car was moving fast. There was no slowing down for intersections or ninety-degree turns. They must be on the highway.

"Is she all right?" she heard the driver ask.

The seat shifted as the heavy man guarding her in the back leaned toward her. She forced her body to involuntarily tip toward the man's weight. Fresh anger rose inside her as his hateful odor filled her nostrils. She fought to keep her breathing steady.

"She's breathing," the man reported in a bored voice.

A fingertip scraped down Bitsy's left breast. Her entire body stiffened.

"She's awake."

She opened her eyes. An inch away was the man's oily smile.

"Rise and shine, sweetheart."

She instructed him to perform a technically physically impossible act on himself.

The driver gave a pitchy laugh. A savage deadness moved into the other man's eyes, made even eerier by the low, amused rumble that rose from him. The tip of his tongue wet his lips as he moved in even closer. "Soon, sugar pie. And thanks to you, it'll be even sweeter." He gave her breast a squeeze, blatant satisfaction filling his fleshy features as he leaned back and lit a cigarette.

Bitsy turned toward the tinted side window. They were heading south down the old coast road, the sea to the right, the mountains to the east. A swirling wall of dense, gray fog had dulled the day's bright glaze. She watched the cars they passed, knowing they could not see her behind the tinted glass. She thought of Mick. Was he alive? Had he heard the noise in the garage and hidden? Had the men searched the house? Or had they come for her only? Perhaps they didn't know yet Mick was still alive. He had said he'd been set up. Perhaps her captors had been sent to take care of her, not knowing their original target was still running around. Either way, what Mick had said was true. She was in danger.

Fresh anger surged through her. How had this happened? She had been so careful, minding her own business, not bothering anyone and only expecting the same courtesy in return.

She glanced at the thug beside her, staring out the window as if this were no more than a Sunday drive. She welcomed the white heat of resolve as her fear segued into anger. The steel core of control returned, clearing her head. She had to get back to Canaan, to Memorial Manor and the safety of her small-scale existence.

She had to get home.

She squirmed against the tight muscles in her upper back, and there, on her right hip she felt it—the barest weight of thin metal. The scalpel still in her lab jacket pocket. She went still. Carefully, staring straight ahead, her clasped hands began pulling the right side of her jacket behind her, quarter inch by quarter inch, until she felt the scalpel beneath her fingers like a magic wand.

"What do you want with me?" She twisted in her seat and stared boldly at the mound of a man next to her. But all her focus was concentrated on the small of her back, where her wrists met and rubbed, soundless millimeter by millimeter, against the blade of the scalpel.

"Besides the usual rape and torture?" The man beside her folded his thick arms across his chest and smiled, pleased with himself. Bitsy glanced at the rearview mirror and caught a flicker of distaste skitter across the driver's features. He did not enjoy the base nature of his work as much as the Cro-

Magnon beside her, she realized, filing the fact away for future reference.

She smiled back sweetly at the man beside her. "Been in the thug business long?"

"You know a man named Michael James?" the driver asked.

He'd taken Bitsy off guard. The constant motion of her bound wrists stopped. He glanced at her in the mirror, a disturbing colorlessness to his eyes.

"Not personally."

The driver's pale gaze stayed on hers in the mirror. "But you do know him?

"His body was brought to Memorial Manor last night."

One pale eyebrow lifted. "He was dead?"

"The majority of our customers are."

The man beside her snorted.

"What happened to the body?" the driver asked, unamused.

"My area is hair and makeup. I only assist with the embalming when we're backed up."

"So you don't know anything about Michael James? Goes by 'Mick.'"

"Just that he's dead."

The driver smiled cruelly in the mirror. "That's not what you told the police."

The man beside her leaned in. "Where is he?"

She suddenly wished she knew. She looked away, out the window, but the fog formed a wall between them and the world. In the side mirror, she glimpsed a flash of color in the dense gray. Electric-green. She narrowed her eyes, peering harder into the gloom, uncertain.

"Depends," she said.

"On what?" the man next to her demanded.

She looked pointedly at the flashy gold cross dangling from the man's thick neck. "On what he did during his time here on earth."

The man huffed, but said nothing more. They drove in silence for a short while. Bitsy looked but did not again see the electric-green flash in the fog behind them again and wondered if she had imagined it. With the scalpel, she worked slowly, methodically at the wire fettering her wrists. She focused more on pressure than scraping back and forth, careful not to make any noise.

"Where are we going?" She needed to keep the conversation alive to make sure a sudden scrape would not reveal her activity.

"To meet some people who want to talk to you," her neighbor said.

"They couldn't just call? E-mail?"

The driver smiled. The oaf beside her shook his head but chuckled. Maybe her mother had been wrong when she'd warned repeatedly, "Nobody likes a smart aleck, Bitsy."

Bitsy shifted in her seat and saw the man next to her eye her legs, which were angled at maximum advantage. She fought the urge to twist them away from his leer, but she could feel the give of the wire on her wrists, was certain she was almost to the point of cutting through. She tipped her head to check out the side mirror again. Nothing for several seconds, then she saw it. So far back, she would have missed it if she hadn't been purposefully looking for it. In the grayness was a streak of green. Then it was gone. At that moment, the scalpel sliced through the last filament of wire. Her wrists were free.

"How much longer?" she asked.

"We'll get there when we get there," the man next to her answered.

"Did you go to college?"

"No." He gave her a sidelong glance. "Why?"

She shrugged. "I thought you might have been a philosophy major."

The driver laughed. Her neighbor didn't.

"Wiseass, huh?"

Maybe her mother had been right.

"C'mon, guys. You're not giving me much here."

"It's a two-way street," the driver noted.

She sighed. "I could use a cappuccino."

"A cappuccino?" The man beside her looked at her incredulously.

"Check your Geneva Convention. All captives are entitled to one cappuccino of their choice." She leaned over. "I'm crazy for the fat-free French vanilla."

"You're crazy all right," her kidnapper agreed.

She sank back into the seat. "And a banana nut muffin." She smiled at the man beside her. "I bet you're a bear-claw kind of guy."

"We need gas," the driver said. "If we pass pumps with a convenience store, we'll get some coffees."

She met the driver's gaze in the mirror. She was right about him. He didn't enjoy his line of work like his partner here. Probably preferred to think of himself as the brains. Her hand curled around the scalpel, ready.

Twenty minutes later, they drove into the parking lot of a small, roadside shop. The driver stayed in the car while his partner got out, slamming the car door before moving to the gas tank.

Bitsy sat perfectly still, not wanting to risk drawing any attention and the discovery of the knife. Only her eyes moved, scanning the store and the small lot. Her hand tightened on the scalpel.

The big man finished filling the car. Bitsy watched him move toward the store and disappear through its door.

The driver turned toward her as he said, "All right, let me ask—" But Bitsy was already leaning forward. Wrapping her arm around the driver's neck, she placed the scalpel's razor edge against the thick vein in his throat.

"What the—" The man reached for his gun.

Bitsy pressed the scalpel into the man's flesh. "I know exactly where to cut you so that all your body fluids pour out in exactly six minutes. You'll be dead before your dimwitted buddy gets done blowing the foam off my French vanilla. Now let go of the gun."

The car door suddenly swung open, startling both Bitsy and her captor.

"I'd do what she says, Wiggs," said the voice that had turned Bitsy's world upside down. Mick crouched in the opened doorway, pressed a pistol to the driver's temple. He looked at Bitsy.

"She's brought tougher men than you to their knees."

Chapter Five

Mick grabbed the man's gun, then patted him down for other weapons. "Move over," he ordered. Bitsy held firm as the man slid over, her arm staying wrapped around his neck, the blade angled against the skin stubbly with razor burn.

Mick moved in behind the wheel and shifted the car into gear. The sheet was gone. He was wearing a T-shirt she recognized as an oversize one she favored for pajamas. He made for a sight in the too-tight T-shirt and the too-tight sweatpants. His eyes were red and irritated from the hair spray.

Bitsy heard a yell as he drove the car out of the lot. Glancing back, she saw Wiggs's partner in the store's doorway, a confused expression muddling his fleshy face. A cardboard tray holding covered containers fell from his meat-hook hands. The car shot out of the lot and the tray dropped, liquid splashing, steam rising and the man running now with the awkward lumbering stride of large men, his hand reaching inside his jacket, pulling out the pistol, aiming, but it was too late. The car veered into traffic. The man stopped, became smaller. The car took a curve and the man disappeared.

Mick glanced over at Bitsy. "Hello, love. You look like hell. I like the scalpel though." His gaze flickered to the knife at Wiggs's throat. "Nice touch."

Bitsy sent him a long, hooded gaze that said she was not amused, when the truth hit her as hard as the first time she had looked into those baby blues. He had rescued her. Granted, she had been in the process of saving herself when he had arrived, but, bottom line, he had come. Why? If what he said was true and he was really in as much trouble as he'd told her, he could have used this opportunity to run. Hell, he hadn't even had to come back at all. If the people who were after them were as powerful as he said, the alibi of one woman wouldn't save him. Especially one whose integrity had already been damaged by the Dumonts in retaliation for dragging a member of their dynasty through a public divorce. Mick would have been smarter to run. She knew it, and, she assumed, so did he.

She could almost hear the crack of the first chink in her defenses.

A nibbling ache began in her arm from her white-knuckled clutch on the scalpel. She looked at the gun Mick held on the man. The other he had tucked in his waistband. She had the scalpel, but overall, he definitely had the upper hand. Not that she was going to let him know it.

"What the hell took you so long? Another second and I would have slit his throat, driven home, washed up and still been on time to prep Mr. Feeney for the family viewing this evening."

As she said, "slit his throat," she increased the knife's pressure. She felt the man tense. It felt good. She wanted him to think of her and Mick as partners. For the moment, she preferred Mick did, too. She cocked her head, waiting to see if he bought it.

He flashed her an assessing glance. She read nothing from his expression. She saw the bluish shadows bruising the skin beneath his eyes. If he had slept, it had been little. She herself was running on pure adrenaline now.

"So, is this one of the big, bad wolves you warned me about?" As she spoke, she slid the knife up and down, scraping the man's neck. The lower half of her face felt pulpy from his partner's blows. She was hungry, tired and achy. She was not in a good mood.

"And you," he said, "ran right into their waiting arms. You'll start listening to me now."

"Like hell."

"Wiggs, share with the dubious Bitsy here what you and your ape partner were planning to do to her."

Wiggs answered with a sailor's oath, cursing them both.

Keeping the car's speed steady at sixty-five miles per hour, Mick angled his gun and shot the man's kneecap.

The jolt went right through the man into Bitsy. Only a swift reflex on her part avoided the knife cutting into his throat. The man let out a primal howl. Bitsy kept her grip on the knife, stunned now, watching the blood blackening the man's pant leg.

"The nice thing about .22s, as you well know, Wiggs," Mick said as if purely making conversation, "is they can do a lot of damage without killing you." He aimed it lower. "I'll give you one more chance before I take out the ankle." Mick hadn't looked away from the road once. Until that moment, Bitsy had actually believed she could beat this man.

"Jesus Christ." The man clutched his knee, trying to stem the blood flow. "You know how we work. We supply information. We get a job. We carry it out. We don't ask questions. They leave us alone."

Bitsy and the man waited, tensing their bodies should Mick make good on his threat. The man had begun to sweat, his pain and terror an oily, oniony smell.

"Maybe you better start being a little curious?"

"Christ, word was you were dead last night. Got more friggin' lives than a Siamese."

"What about the raid on the arms ring? What do you hear on the street about that?"

"That's out of my area."

Mick moved the gun closer to the ankle. His gun hand tensed. Fresh sweat shone on Wiggs's face.

"Untouchable. That's what I heard. They gave up a few of the street dealers for the show, but the whole operation has someone watching their back. They've got protection." Wiggs's head rolled on the seat back, a small, sickly grin exposing his teeth. "And it looks like it's your people, cowboy. Not mine."

They had turned off the main coastal road onto the interstate heading inland toward the city. The smell of car exhaust and overpopulation mixed with the smell of the man's blood and sweat. Body fluids, Bitsy thought. The messiest part of the death business.

The man's breaths were heavier, his eyes glazed, as he headed into shock. "They called us in for the dirty work. Especially when things got…" His lips smacked. "Complicated."

Mick eyed him as if trying to decide to believe him or not. "Tell her." He nodded his head toward Bitsy. "Is she number one on the hit parade?"

Wiggs licked his lips, his repulsive smile returning. He nodded. "After you, of course. Although odds are you're in Tijuana by now, downing Cuervo with a *chiquita* on each knee." The man's head rolled back.

"Once the report came back of only one death in the explosion, the word was already across the border."

"You're an international superstar, amigo." The man's eyes closed, but the sneer stayed in place.

"Don't flatter me, Wiggs. How did they tell you to take her out?"

"Accidents happen," he replied with surprising laissez-faire for a man with a bleeding kneecap.

Mick raised the gun to the man's temple. "Did you do Arthur?"

The man's eyes opened, rolled toward Mick. "That was your own brothers, my friend. They did him. Just like they were supposed to do you. They leave the little fishies for us local boys." The man turned suddenly, plucked a kiss close to Bitsy's ear. She pulled back, his callous laughter following her.

"Bitsy, go into his pockets, get his cell phone and wallet."

She unsnaked her arm from around the man's neck, dropping the scalpel into the lab-jacket pocket. She frisked the man, retrieving his cell phone from his jacket's inside breast pocket. His wallet was in his pant's left front pocket.

"Give me the phone," Mick instructed. After she handed it to him, he said, "Open up the wallet. Tell me what he's got."

She unfolded the fine-grain leather wallet, looked inside. "Not much cash. A couple twenties, a ten, some ones." She checked the wallet's other slots. "Credit cards, driver's license. Mr. George Seahorn." She looked questioningly at Mick. She slipped out an ivory business card with black embossed lettering. "'Seahorn Coastal Specialties,'" she read. "'Fresh daily.' Who the hell are you guys?"

"What about an ATM card?" Mick ignored her question.

She drew out a plastic gold card. "Bank of California MasterCard."

"That will do. Hang on to the card. Give me the

wallet. I need a little loan, Wiggs. Walking-around money."

Wiggs's eyes did not open.

"I'll get the money back to you."

Wiggs turned his head to Mick, opened his eyes. "You won't live that long."

Mick gave him a smile reminiscent of Wiggs's own snide grin. "I'm a Siamese, remember?"

"Yeah, right." Wiggs rolled his head back onto the seat. His voice was fainter, his complexion pasty. Sweat moistened his skin, but he kept licking his lips as if they were dry. His expression had taken on a distant blankness. Bitsy wondered how long it would be before he passed out from pain.

They took the next exit into the city outskirts, driving in silence except for the scrape of the scalpel against the wire fettering Bitsy's ankles. When her legs where finally free, she slipped the blade back into her jacket pocket as Mick turned into a branch of Bank of California and pulled up alongside the drive-up ATM machine until it was even with the back passenger window. He jammed the gun into Wiggs's groin. "Take an irregular breath, and you'll be singing for the Vienna Boys' Choir." Even Bitsy squirmed.

Mick glanced back at her. His other arm snaked through the front bucket seats, the second gun aimed at her. "Take out the scalpel."

"What are you going to do?"

"Nothing. As long as you do what I tell you."

She fished in her pocket, pulled out the instrument, her eyes never leaving Mick's.

"Move over to the window." Bitsy did as Mick instructed, her eyes still on him, but conscious of the gun. "Open the back window."

She pushed the button. The window slid down.

"Drop the knife out the window."

She reached out the window.

"That's far enough. Drop it."

It landed with a faint clatter.

"Take out the ATM card. Put it in the machine. What's the PIN?" he asked Wiggs.

"Nine-zero-two-two."

"Check the balance first." Mick told her.

The gun was at her back now, grazing the line of her spine. She punched in the numbers. All the time, her mind was working. A way out… She had to find a way out. A large number appeared on the screen.

"Damn, Wiggs," Mick said, when the figure appeared.

"You're in the wrong business," Wiggs said.

Bitsy's hand moved to the door lock. The ATM screen asked, "Would you like to make another transaction?"

"Make a withdrawal. What's the maximum allowed?" Mick asked Wiggs.

"Two hundred."

"Punch in five hundred," Mick told Bitsy.

She pressed the Yes button. Her other hand wrapped around the door lock, waiting. She hit another button, then put in the PIN and waited. The ATM began to whir. When the cash appeared, Bitsy unlocked the door. She reached for the money with one hand, closed her fingers around the door handle with the other. As she took the cash, she pulled back the handle and propelled her body against the door, her shoulder hitting hard. Her body bounced back. The door didn't open.

"Tell her, Wiggs," Mick said in a resigned voice as he pushed a button and the window slid up and sealed.

"The child safety locks are on. My partner switched the one on that door when he got out at the gas station." Wiggs moistened his lips, his head still back against the headrest, his eyes closed. "The back doors can only be opened from the outside."

Mick gazed at her, disappointed. "Give me the cash."

He took the money and stuffed it into the driver door's side panel. He put the car into gear and merged back into traffic, accelerating. Bitsy slumped against the backseat, sitting in silence. She noticed Wiggs's head fell forward onto his chest and almost envied him his respite. Mick took several turns, taking them deeper into the city instead of back to the interstate as she had expected.

She leaned forward between the two front seats. If the sudden movement made any impact, Mick did not show it. He drove, one hand on the wheel, the other still holding the gun on Wiggs. Wiggs's breathing was laden but regular.

"Sit back," he said, his tone bored.

"Why did you come back for me?"

"I'm a sucker for vampire vixens."

"I want to know." She had laid her hand on the center console between the two seats. He glanced at it, at the red lines where the wire had cut into her skin.

"I told you." He looked away from her wrists. "I need you."

"As an alibi?"

"Yes." He stopped for a red light. "And you need me."

"What for?"

He looked back into her eyes. "To keep you alive. Like it or not, darling, right now, I'm your best friend. The sooner you learn that, the easier this will be on us both."

A horn honked. The light had gone green.

Mick pressed on the accelerator and moved the car through the intersection.

"Do you really believe the word of one woman can save you?"

"No. But like it or not, you're all I've got right now, too."

They drove down into a no-man's-land of abandoned warehouses and chain-link fences. Mick pulled to the curb of a wide parking lot overgrown with weeds. He looked over at Wiggs. The man's eyes were open but unfocused.

Mick unlocked the passenger door. "All right, Wiggs, end of the road. Get out."

Wiggs looked at his captor. "You gonna kill me, Mick?"

"Not today."

Wiggs opened the door and looked back before he slid out. "They're going to kill you, Mick. You know that."

"Not today," Mick repeated.

The man smiled weakly, then got out of the car.

"Wiggs?"

The man leaned in, supporting himself on the doorjamb, standing on one leg.

"I'll pop the trunk. There's a black disk-shaped object about the size of a quarter in the wheel well. Take it out."

Dragging his left leg, using the car for support, Wiggs hobbled to the back of the car. Several seconds later, he closed the trunk lid. Through the rear window, he held up the small disk. Mick nodded and pulled away, heading west. Bitsy looked back. Wiggs had staggered a few steps, was resting against a pole. When she turned back, she saw Mick watching her in the mirror.

"He would have killed you," he said.

"So you keep telling me."

"Actually his boyfriend would have done you. They run a two-bit drug operation out of a storefront down on the wharf. Last job they had was a hacker who came too close to Agency files. He was found gutted like a fish."

She showed no reaction as her stomach turned inside out. "Bull."

He shrugged. "Believe what you want but in some cultures, you would be my love slave for life in repayment for what I just did for you."

"Kidnapped me? At gunpoint?"

"I saved your life."

"Tell that to a jury." Past the tinted window, she saw the traffic sign for a hospital and realized Mick had dropped Wiggs only a few blocks away. Coincidence? Or compassion?

"What was that thing in the trunk?"

"A tracker. We may have company soon. But first they'll find Wiggs."

He flipped open the cell phone, jabbed the buttons, waited for someone to pick up on the other end. "I've got the girl." He paused. "This was the wrong time to start underestimating me. I'll be in touch."

He ended the call, then immediately punched in another number.

"Give me Smiley." A pause, then he said, "It's me. I have something for you. A trade." Mick chuckled low at something said on the other end of the line. "You'll like this one. Don't bring anything fancy. And four cell phones. You know where to find me. Forty-five minutes tops." He flipped the phone closed and threw it out the window.

"Who's Smiley?" Bitsy asked.

Mick ignored her.

"Who was that you called first?"

"An old boss." He didn't elaborate.

"Where are we going now?"

He didn't answer.

"To meet Smiley, right?" She filled in the blanks. "And make a trade. What are we trading?" She leaned forward, came in close. "You do have a plan, don't you, Mick?"

"Sit back and shut up," he growled.

"Why? What are you going to do if I don't? Shoot me?"

His glance grazed her. "I'm not going to hurt you, Bitsy."

"Great." The word rang out like a slap. "I'm glad we cleared that up. Because you know, the abduction at gunpoint caused me a little concern."

He watched her in the mirror.

"I do have one question though." She flattened the rising hysterical lilt in her voice. "If you're not going to kill me, Mick, what are you going to do with me?"

He looked at her, his smile slow. "I told you. I'm going to save you, Bitsy Leigh…and you're going to save me."

"Exactly what are you going to save me from? More friends of yours like the one we just left?"

Mick's mouth tightened. "Amateurs like that, they're the least of your worries."

She studied his profile, the high forehead, the close-cropped hair, the hard expression. A shadow of a beard had begun to darken his cheeks. "Who should I be worried about?"

His gaze, the blue base of a flame, went to her again. The car made a smooth turn. Inside the tinted glass, it was quiet. Bitsy heard only the skip and play of her thoughts. When she thought he wasn't going to say anything more, he spoke so suddenly, she started.

"A Californian congressman was shot last night around nine-thirty."

She looked at him. "Congressman Kittredge." He wasn't looking at her.

"They're going to say I did it."

"Last night at nine-thirty you were at Memorial Manor."

"Only you and one other person will swear to that." Mick looked at her. "That other person was killed last night."

Her breath drew inward, her thoughts dizzying as if she were in a whirlpool, being sucked under.

"You're my alibi. I need you alive. They want you dead."

The distance between her world today and yesterday continued widening. "They? Who are 'they'?"

"The people I worked for."

"Who did you work for?"

A corner of his mouth tipped up like a twitch at first, then widening into a smile, full and frightening. "The United States government."

She stared at him, waiting for him to explain and at the same time trying to gauge the level of his sanity. Several minutes lapsed before he began to talk again.

"In the late forties, during the Cold War, the government created the Agency of Policy Coordination. Its official purpose was to carry out conventional intelligence activity—surveillance, information gathering, analysis. Its real purpose was to serve as a cover, channeling funding and manpower for programs that operated outside the normal order of things."

"'Outside the normal order of things'?" she echoed.

"Not subject to public scrutiny, administrative regulation, constitutional interference. Programs free to proceed secretly and without fear of consequences."

"That sounds illegal."

"A matter of perspective."

Bitsy looked out, past Mick, through the tinted glass. She weighed his words. They had long left the fog behind, but the sun was blocked out by tall buildings and cloud cover. Inside the car stayed shadowed. "And you work for this…secret organization?"

"I did…" Her captor's gaze fell on her. "Until last night. I was recruited in my twenties by a man named Arthur Prescott."

She remembered Mick had accused Wiggs of "doing" someone named Arthur. "And he was killed last night?"

"Trying to save me."

"If what you say is true, then the congressman who was shot…he was shot by his own government?"

Mick nodded.

"Why?"

Determination steeled Mick's features. "That's what I plan to find out. All I know now is we're next on the list."

Bitsy sat back against the seat, rubbing the back of her neck as if to eliminate the confusion. Her thoughts stayed thick and murky. "Secret agents? Government conspiracies?" She studied him. She'd read about people like him. "Do you hear voices, too?"

He laughed. It was such a normal sound.

"You expect me to believe that the federal government is killing its own citizens?"

His voice was calm, quiet, no more than a lullaby. "Not the whole federal government, but someone in it. Someone with authority issued those orders last night. I don't expect you to believe it. That's why I had to abduct you first and explain later."

In his low timbre of reason, he said, "But it's the truth."

She stared at him. She almost wanted to believe him.

"I know you're scared of me," he continued in a lulling tone. "But at the moment I'm your best friend. You're all I've got right now...." He steered past a sharp corner, then looked at her. "And, like it or not, I'm all you've got."

He moved his gaze back to the road. "You won't get hurt as long as you cooperate."

He didn't look at her, but still, a shudder passed through her. He was clever, plying her with his fanciful tales and a false sense of protection. Cold and clever and calculating.

Of course, he needed her cooperation. They were on the interstate again, heading away from the city, passing the suburban sprawl outside its limits. Somewhere with people to cry out to, run to…unless you believed your savior sat right here beside you, perversely enjoying his sham.

Her fear transformed once more, plummeted, became leaden. Her false hero had just made a fatal mistake. She now despised him as much as feared him. And this hot coil of hatred was a weapon much more powerful than the scalpel she'd wielded or the gun held easily in his hand.

"I'll bring you home, Bitsy. I promise." His eyes were too blue to be believed. The coil inside her tightened.

"You know what I think? I think one of us is crazy here, but I'm not sure who—you or me?" She forced her voice to sound vulnerable. She'd been a victim once before. Never again.

Mick looked at her. "At this moment, it's a draw."

Chapter Six

Bitsy laughed.

"You know, I almost believe you." Two could play this game. She'd seduce him into the same illusion of security. She'd be so ready, willing and able to co-operate then by the time they got to the first town, he'd be calling her Bonnie and she'd be calling him Clyde. Then, when his smile was soft and his head turned, she would make her move.

She smiled at him now. Not too broadly, just a tentative quarter curve of possible trust. After she'd tried to escape at the house, he wouldn't be easily fooled by an abrupt capitulation on her part. Suspicion and skepticism even now sharpened his features.

But when he spoke, she heard again that soothing current that, under the circumstances, was chilling instead of comforting. "You don't have to believe me. You only have to not pull any more stunts like you did back at your house. I'll take care of everything else." He glanced at her. "Everything will be fine."

Shoot, now she actually did want to believe him. "Okay," she agreed, lying through her teeth.

He turned off the main road onto a narrower road, the landscape flattened by wide expanses of nothingness. They had long left the sea and San Francisco and were heading north toward the mountains. Traffic was steady but light. They passed houses set back, growing farther and farther apart. Mick took a left onto another narrower, bumpier road. They topped a rise, and there, down below, was a bowl of a valley. Tall pines and a lake with the morning mist still not burned off it yet. Mick aimed the car toward it, following the road that curved and dipped around the water. Bitsy glimpsed the rough logs of small square cabins among the tall pines. They drove around the lake to the other side. A quarter of a mile later, Mick pulled into a gravelly lot with an abandoned flat-roofed building in its center. In one cloudy window, a small rectangular sign said OFFICE. Twelve faded turquoise doors with brass-plated numbers were evenly spaced along the rest of the former motel. Rusted iron fencing edged the concrete walk along the building's length. A sign, eroded by weather and age, pronounced this to be Long Lake Motel. A narrower, rectangular sign half hung from its bottom. Vacancies.

Mick drove around to the back, parked, cut the engine and pocketed the keys. Bitsy looked at him with a raised brow. "Is this where we meet Smiley?" she asked optimistically. He had said he wasn't going to kill her. She hadn't thought to ask about rape and torture.

He pulled out the gun and her optimism faded. Fresh terror took its place.

"I'll get out first." He gestured with the gun toward the building. "Try anything stupid and I'll shoot you. Not to kill you. But to stop you."

The image of Wiggs's exploded kneecap flashed in her mind. She thought of the grotesque blue doors, trying not to think what might lie behind them. They were miles from anywhere, with no one to hear her screams. All her bravado from only minutes ago dissolved. Mick had opened the door, was rounding the front of the car. Another second and he would be at her side. And she, at his mercy once more.

Her door opened. She only had one choice.

"No-o-o-o!" With the roar of a woman brought to the brink, she sprang at her captor. The unexpected force of her full-body slam rammed Mick against the passenger side door. Her leg lashed upward, her spiked heel catching him full force in the groin with every ounce of strength she had. Then she was gone, not even turning to see if he was on his knees. She heard his curses the same time as the shots, peppering pops. She dove, a sudden, wrenching tear along the back length of her thigh. She rolled, bullets piercing the ground, ringing out around her, sending up puffs of dirt and pine needles. She crawled behind a slender pine and, sitting up, leaned against its trunk, heaving. She looked down, checking her body. No blood. No punctures from speeding steel. Just a fiery pain along the back of her right leg when she tried to bend her knee. She must have torn her hamstring again.

He'd be on her soon. She had to get up, get going. She stood, but pain turned her vision black, forced her back down.

"Hell, lady," Mick yelled as he rounded the tree. He looked down at her, disgusted. "I'm all done." He crouched, his face inches from hers. "Go. You want to die that bad, go. Run right back and find out who the enemy really is."

He stalked off. She rubbed her thigh, the pain pulsing in fresh waves. Her stockings had ripped when she'd fallen. She tore them off and carrying her heels in one hand and favoring her uninjured leg, tried to get up. She took two hops, sank back down. Exhaustion, frustration, pain overwhelmed her. Through the haze, an observation sprang up. He hadn't shot her. He had shot *at* her, but he hadn't shot her. He may have missed but, if he was a trained secret operative, he would know how to shoot to kill…or at least, maim. Either his story about being a secret agent was the bunk she'd suspected or…

A shadow fell across her. She looked up. He towered over her, his face still twisted with disdain. With the back of her hand, she swiped at the tears streaking her face.

"What?" he snapped. "What now? I told you. Get

out of here. I won't stop you. You're on your own now. And, God help you, I take no responsibility for what happens." He folded his arms across his chest, waited. She turned her head away.

"Go," he ordered.

She whipped her head back around. "I can't," she spat out angrily.

"Why not?" he demanded.

She tried to bend her leg and stopped halfway. Along the back of her thigh, the skin had already begun to balloon and turn mottled.

Swearing, he squatted down. His touch was gentle as he examined the bruising skin. Still she winced.

"I tore my hamstring about a month ago."

His gaze met hers. "Can you put any weight on it?"

"A little. It hurts like the devil."

"The original pull probably hadn't completely healed, and your little getaway ripped it again."

She looked past him to a sign with a credit-card logo hanging about four feet up off a pole stuck into the edge of the motel's property. The sign was less than two feet square and about two hundred feet away. "See that red circle on that sign?" she said.

He looked over his shoulder in the direction of her gaze. He looked back at her. "Yeah, why?"

"Do me a favor. Shoot a hole through its center."

He studied her as if assessing her state of mind. "Why?"

"Just do it."

He slipped the pistol from where he had holstered

it, took aim and fired. The sign swung crazily for several minutes. When it slowed, Bitsy saw the perfect round hole in the center of the red circle.

She looked at Mick. He shot like a trained machine. "You missed me deliberately."

He didn't answer. He merely reholstered the gun and stood. "I told you. If I was going to kill you, you would already be dead."

For the first time, she believed him. He leaned down and gathered her in his arms.

Her body tensed. "What are you doing?"

"Shut up. Wrap your arms around my neck." In no position to argue, she did as he said. He lifted her effortlessly and carried her toward the motel.

Stopping before room number four, he kicked open the door. Scurrying sounds in the walls greeted them. The door swung back, revealing one wide room dominated by a bed with a thin, gnawed coverlet in mustard-gold and yellowed-white paisley print. Mick set her on top of it. She leaned back against the bare wall. There was no headboard. The worn curtains sagging at the windows were pulled closed, dimming any light attempting to make its way in. The room smelled like a storage closet.

"Not exactly the Beverly Wilshire," Bitsy observed, her nose wrinkling. Still, although the mattress was thin, it was more comfortable than the hard ground. "How did you find this hot spot?"

Mick didn't answer. He slipped off her heels, grabbed one of the two flat pillows on the bed and shook it out of its stained case. "Can you bend your leg a little?"

She slowly angled her knee. His hand slid to the back of her knee, supporting it. He watched her face, but she fought to keep her expression neutral. He wrapped the pillowcase around her thigh tight enough to give support but not decrease circulation. He doubled the pillows and propped them under her knee. "Relax your leg," he said.

She eased her leg onto the pillows. She flinched. He studied her.

"It only really hurts when I bend my knee. I'll be fine."

"Rest now," he ordered. "Keep it elevated." He walked into the bathroom. As he was opening the door, Bitsy called his name. He turned and looked at her over his shoulder.

"Thank you."

He headed into the bathroom, closing the door behind him.

When he came out, he sat down in a cheap vinyl armchair tilted to one side where one of the four short legs had broken off.

"What do we do now?"

He tipped his head back, closed his eyes. "We wait."

Bitsy tapped her fingers on the coverlet. After a few seconds of silence, she said, "Your friend knows how to get here?"

"He knows. And he's not a friend."

Mick stretched out his legs, the too-short sweatpants rising higher, revealing toned calves. The rest of his body was trim and muscular as if daily workouts were mandatory. His face, even in repose, maintained an infuriating arrogance.

"This Smiley character—is he a secret agent, too?"

"No." Mick revealed nothing further.

"Who is he then?"

One eye squinted open. "You ask an awful lot of questions." The eye closed.

"What are you going to do? Shoot me?"

"Afraid I already blew that chance."

She suppressed a smile even though his eyes stayed closed. "When Smiley," she deliberately distorted the name, "gets here, what are we going to do next?"

Mick sighed. "You'll see. Now shut up for a few minutes."

She shifted her weight on the thin mattress, gingerly readjusting the position of her thigh. She looked around the bare room. Her fatigue had gone beyond exhaustion to a twilight state between sleep and consciousness. This hazy perception partnered perfectly with her current surroundings and the unexpected events of the last sixteen hours.

The silence began to claw at her. "I'm starving," she announced. No response from James Bond. She watched the rise and fall of his chest, wondering if he was asleep. Even if he was, her hamstring would make it difficult to get far on foot. The car keys were in his pants pocket, the guns tucked or holstered.

Aggravation seemed to be her only weapon at the moment.

"How much longer until your buddy arrives? That is if he does arrive."

"Am I going to have to gag you?" Mick growled.

Before Bitsy could respond, she heard the crunch of tires on the gravel. Mick shot out of the chair, went to the window, lifting the curtain enough to look out. A car door slammed and seconds later, there was a knock at the door. Mick peered through the peephole and smiled as he swung open the door.

A large black man with the meanest countenance Bitsy had ever encountered filled the doorway. He was wearing a cheap suit and a scowl. Hence, Bitsy deducted, "Smiley."

The man stepped into the room, glanced at Bitsy, his expression not changing. "Where's the trade, Rapp?"

Rapp? Bitsy glanced at the man she knew as Mick James. His attention was on Smiley.

"Out back. 525 BMW."

If Smiley was impressed, he wasn't showing it.

"It'll need a little clean up," Mick added.

Smiley's blasé expression said, "What else is new?" Aloud, he said, "You see the trade?"

Mick nodded. "Nice and dull. It'll do fine. You have any trouble getting here?"

"No, and I don't expect any. The fenced phones are in the glove compartment. All former vacation models from burglaries of people out of town. The accounts are set up under aliases."

"What about pharmaceuticals?"

Smiley lifted a brow. Mick jerked his head toward Bitsy propped up on the bed. "Had a little fall."

Smiley quirked his other brow but didn't look at Bitsy.

"Nothing exotic," Mick said. "Ibuprofen, aspirin, something to take the edge off."

Smiley reached inside his jacket pocket, pulled out a medicine vial and handed it to Mick. "Vicodin." His scowl deepened. "On every corner like candy."

"That will certainly take the edge off." Mick reached for the bottle. "Nothing milder?"

"Back in my desk drawer. Give her a half a pill. She'll be fine."

Mick opened the vial, shook out a pill, set it on the scratched stand next to the bed. "Take only a half. I'll be right back."

"I'll be waiting with bated breath." To her surprise, Smiley, who still hadn't looked at her, released a low rumble.

"You finally got a live one, huh, Rapp?"

"Stay out of my love life, Smiley," Mick said as he opened the door for the big man and followed him out into the parking lot.

Ignoring the pill, Bitsy carefully swung her legs over the side of the bed and hopped to the closest window to peek out. Mick and Smiley got into a nondescript four-door hatchback and drove around to the back of the building where the other car was parked. Standing on one foot, she watched out the window until her good leg began to ache. She gingerly lowered her other foot to the floor. She shifted her weight to the injured leg and took a step. Pain spasmed along the back of her thigh. She waited until it subsided, then took another step. More pain, but not as severe as the first step. She breathed in and limped back to the bed, hopping the last two steps. She sat down, fresh sweat beading on her upper lip and down her spine. She refused to succumb to help-lessness, but she did have to admit, the hamstring might slow her down.

She waited. Several minutes passed and Mick or whatever the hell his name was hadn't returned. And what about this Smiley character? Not her typical idea of a secret operative.

More minutes passed. Bitsy listened, thought she heard a car drive out, then another. She scrambled to her feet, ignoring the pain as she hobbled to the window as quickly as her injury would allow and looked out only to see the back end of the hatchback driving away. The BMW was already out of sight.

She muttered every curse word she could think of and then added a few more she made up. Control was not a priority at the moment. The bastard had left her.

He'd terrorized her, hauled her off at gunpoint to God knows where, shot at her, and then, when she was at her weakest, he'd run off, abandoning her to fate and whatever fun was in store for her.

Men.

C'mon, Bitsy, the voice of reason, made tiny by

her rage, spoke. *The guy carries a gun and shoots people willy-nilly in the kneecap. Did you expect different?*

She half hopped, half hobbled back to the bed and sank down. The worst thing was a small part of her had begun to trust him. When was she going to learn?

At least, she was free. Although how much good that would do her out in the wilds with a torn hamstring, she wasn't sure. But it was over. She was no longer at his mercy.

She stood on her good leg, tested her other. Pain pulsed as she fully straightened it and took several steps, but she could bear it. If she could get to the road, she could flag someone down, get help. She sat on the bed, picked up one shoe and with a sharp twist, broke off the heel. She did the same to the other and slipped them on. With an awkward gait favoring her good leg, she headed outside, her progress slow but steady. As she started across the lot, her eyes scanned her surroundings until she found what she wanted. A branch with a sufficient circumference hung low enough for her to reach. She moved toward it with her unwieldy gait and bent it up and down and side to side until it snapped. Leaning her weight on the branch, she headed toward the road.

Her speed was maddeningly slow, and even putting as little weight as possible on her injured limb, the pain was constant. Several times, she stopped to catch her breath. She had only gone a quarter mile when she heard the sound of tires coming down the road. The hatchback headed straight at her. She did not have time to examine her reaction. It was futile to look for someplace to hide. Her former captor behind the wheel had already seen her. She looked straight ahead, focused on the horizon and placed one foot in front of the other, trying to keep her walk as normal as possible.

Mick slowed the car to an idle and opened the window. "Get in," he said.

She wished she could march away but had to settle for a small hop. Mick eased the car forward to keep even with her.

"Get in."

She tipped her chin up. "I don't think you're the guilty-conscience type, so I'm assuming you came back because you hadn't tortured me enough."

"We're wasting time here. Time we don't have."

She kept moving forward.

"I've got food."

The man was shameless.

"There's a small store two miles away."

"I'm not hungry," she lied.

"They got a little deli where you can get sandwiches." Mick held up a triangular sandwich half on what looked like rye bread with a lettuce leaf with a blob of mayo hanging out one end and took a big bite.

"You like turkey and Swiss or Italian mix?" he said between chews.

Her stomach growled. Her steps slowed. "Just throw one out at me like you would to a caged lion."

"Yeah, then what?" He took another bite, raised a bottle to his lips and drank greedily. "The nearest road is a while yet."

"I'll be fine."

"Going to flag someone down? What type of individual do you expect to stop for a crazy-looking hitchhiker in black leather and theatrical makeup out in the middle of nowhere?"

"A good Samaritan."

"My money says it will be someone who is looking for a piece of action and believes his prayers have been heard and answered by the devil himself."

She shot him a dirty glance.

He took a large bite. "At least with me, you know what kind of trouble you're in. Someone else? Who knows? Could be crazier than me."

"I'll take those chances, Mick or Rapp or whatever the hell your name is."

"I have aliases, networks I've formed, people I know I can call exactly in case of a situation like this. Smiley knows me as someone else for his own protection."

"What's your real name?"

"I don't know."

She shot him a skeptical glance.

"Legally I'm John Smith. The State chose it for me."

"Where were your parents?"

"Good question."

"They weren't around?"

"No."

"Who's Mick James?"

"No one. A spook. Until last night."

She stabbed the stick into the ground. "Who's Smiley?"

"A city detective."

She threw him a skeptical sidelong glance.

"He hates the feds."

"He helped you."

"I'm not a fed. I'm nothing, I don't exist." The car inched forward, staying even with her awkward progress. "They didn't have elastic bandages or anything like that at the store, but they did have a small employee first-aid kit I persuaded them to part with."

She scowled. "What did you do? Shoot out a few kneecaps?"

He didn't even blink. "No, I paid them for it."

"You're a real prince."

"Every girl's dream. Stop wasting my time with the obvious and get in this car."

She stopped a minute, jabbed her stick into the ground and faced him. "Do you really think I'm going to voluntarily get back into a car with a criminal?"

"I'd say you've got no other choice. And I'm not a criminal."

"No, everybody runs around taking people against their will."

"Hey, you were pretty handy with that scalpel."

"That was self-defense."

"Same coin, different sides."

Her features tightened with impatience. "What's that supposed to mean?"

"Listen, I'm not wasting any more time. Get in the car."

"You ran out on me," she accused.

"I couldn't trust you to behave yourself in the car while I was inside the store."

"You could have, at least, told me where you were going."

"Then you would have wanted to go. I'd have to say no. I wasn't going to waste time arguing. I'm not going to waste any more time now." He stopped the car. "Get in the damn car."

"Go to hell."

He clutched the steering wheel so hard, Bitsy thought the plastic would break in two.

"I'll count to three. One…"

"Don't bother. Go."

There was only silence for a moment as if the world were holding its breath. Mick punched the gas, gunned the engine and the car shot forward, spraying up dust and dirt.

Bitsy stared after the speeding car. "The son of a bitch left me."

HE TOLD HIMSELF TO EASE UP, slow down, but anger kept his foot pressing the gas pedal to the floor. A burning clutched his chest, his breath came out raggedly. No one could make him lose control like this except a damn woman. And not any woman.

This damn woman.

Mick clutched the steering wheel until his knuckles whitened. Looking in the mirror, he saw, through the dust and dirt, Bitsy standing in the road, feet planted, giving him the middle finger.

And he laughed like the child he'd never been.

He cursed her once more as he slammed on the brakes. He shifted into Reverse and shot back toward the woman with her arm still uplifted and her finger pointed skyward.

Bitsy watched the hatchback reverse, its swaying tail end heading toward her. She half loped, half stumbled toward the woods, while trying to look over her shoulder. The car squealed to a stop. Leaving the engine running, Mick leaped out of the car and bounded toward her. Wrapping his arms around her waist, he slung her over his shoulder. Her fists beat his back, her feet aimed for his chest but his hold was too strong. He carried her to the driver's side and dropped her across the front seat. Her back landed against the passenger door. Her feet flailed at him, ignoring the pain in her leg.

He reached out and grabbed a fist of her hair.

She yelped with pain and surprise, involuntarily turning toward him, trying to ease the tension across her scalp. She felt hair ripping from her scalp. Her body wrenched away, only increasing the pain. "Let go, you big bully."

"I've had mobsters that were less trouble than you, lady."

"Well, get used to it, bucko," she said, her body twisting wildly, "because this is only the beginning."

"Bring it on," Mick coolly advised, steering with one hand.

She fought, flopping like a hooked fish for a few minutes more, then she went still. The contrast was so keen, Mick eyed her, his brow furrowed. Her body deflated like a popped balloon. She slumped beside him. Not trusting her tricks, he tightened his fist in her hair and tugged her closer to him.

"You win," she said.

He rolled his eyes, his fist clenching her hair. "I'm not the opponent, Bitsy."

"You're not exactly the ally."

"And you're not exactly a walk in the park." He glanced at her, grateful that she had stopped struggling but not certain if this new version was any better.

She heaved a sigh, her body collapsing into an even more pitiful posture. "I only have one question."

He waited.

"Why now? Can someone answer me that?"

"Why now what?" He kept his eyes on the road, his hand wound in her hair.

"Why now?" she repeated stubbornly. "Why now after years of searching and self-flagellation and sessions on the couch, after self-hypnosis tapes, Dr. Phil and trying to breathe through my eyelids."

She paused. Mick opened his mouth but before he could ask her what the heck she was talking about, she began again.

"I once drank nothing but carrot juice for a week. I've endured underwire bras and thong underwear and saying no to sex until I thought I found the 'one.'" Her fingers made quotation marks in the air. "Only to find the 'one' was just like anyone else, except maybe a bit more cruel."

She paused again, her expression thoughtful as if considering something. "So I only have one question. Why now? Why now do the fates decide to kill me? Why didn't they just do it when I was thirteen and I could have avoided fourteen years of torture?"

Mick released a genuine laugh. She looked over at him. She wasn't laughing.

"Bitsy, Bitsy, Bitsy." He said her name with a musical lilt as he shook his head and smiled. His gaze met hers. "No one is going to kill you," he said softly. "I promise."

For the second time that day, he had made her believe him.

"Will you let go of my hair?" If she saw an opportunity, she had to take it.

"No." But his arm had slackened and the pain along her scalp was gone.

"Would you stretch your arm out far enough so I can reach that sandwich on the floor?" The bag of purchases from the store had taken a nosedive off the front passenger seat during the scuffle and had landed on the floor.

He glanced down at her. She was not above making her eyes doe-like. He stretched out his arm.

She reached and grabbed the other half of the thick sandwich with lettuce and turkey hanging out the sides of the bread. She settled back, unwrapping the cellophane, and chomped down. "Good," she said between chews, her mouth full.

She took several more bites. Mouth bulging, she observed, "You came back for me."

He didn't comment.

"Why?"

"I'm a masochist."

"We all are on some level." She chewed, swallowed. "Really, I know there's the alibi thing, but, I hate to be the one to break it to you, you'd have a better chance if you disappeared than depending on the statement of one woman versus the United States government. If I'm as much trouble as you insist I am, why didn't you take off and leave me to fend for myself in the wilds of East Bejesus?"

She wished she didn't witness the stark sorrow that flashed in his eyes. It was less than a second, but in that moment, she saw something so strong, powerful and wrenching, she knew his answer before he gave it voice.

"You left someone before, and the person died?" she questioned quietly.

"I didn't leave her."

"But she died?"

He nodded. "Because of me."

"Who was she?"

"It was a long time ago. It doesn't matter."

"It seems to me that for you, it's all that does matter."

His eyes on the road and his hands white knuckled on the wheel, he answered, "My wife."

He faced Bitsy. "She was my wife."

Chapter Seven

"Now drop it," he ordered.

Bitsy complied, not because she wasn't curious and didn't feel she had the right to pry in the man's personal life. Forget that. You pointed a gun at someone, you crossed a line and the common boundaries of polite society no longer applied.

No, she suppressed the questions percolating inside her like the aftereffects of Aunt Charlene's five-star chili, because she was afraid to know this man's sad story. Once revealed, he would no longer be the corpse who'd risen from the dead, larger than life, and had sent her world into a maelstrom of guns and goons and getaways. He would be a man of flesh and bone, with sorrows and triumphs. He would become human. And even more dangerous.

"So, now what?" She took another bite of sandwich and propped her foot with the injured hamstring on the edge of the car window. His fingers remained tangled in her hair but had eased to almost an affectionate gesture.

"We're going to meet someone."

"The person you called from my house? Another member of Mick James's secret society?"

"Someone willing to help us."

"Why?"

Mick shook his head. "Do you have to know everything?"

"Considering the current situation, I'm a big fan of being informed."

He shook his head again, but his impatience slackened to acceptance. "I've had three people believe in me," he said. "Two are dead. The person we are going to meet is the third."

"Where are we meeting this person?"

"Near the Nevada state line."

"When?"

"Tonight, if all goes well."

"How is this person going to help us?"

"I need information. This person can get it."

Bitsy readjusted her foot and leaned back against the seat. Without a word, Mick's hand slid from her hair.

She made no comment, not wanting to jinx her freedom. "I wonder if anyone knows I'm missing yet."

Mick said nothing.

"I don't want them to be worried. They don't know that I'm safe and sound here with you. That I would be in more danger if I was home with them. Of course, I was on call today. Unless there were new deliveries, I wouldn't be expected in until tomorrow. If there was nothing in the news yet, and Lanie calls and gets my machine, she'll figure I'm…um, occupied."

"No," Mick said.

"I didn't ask you anything."

"You were about to."

"Is that so? What, pray tell, was I about to ask you?"

"If you could call your cousin."

"Ha! I know you wouldn't let me do that." She sent him a sidelong glance. "Would you?"

"No. They'll be monitoring your cousin's incoming and outgoing calls. If they think she knows something or could be useful to them, they'll involve her."

"Here I thought it was because you don't trust me."

"That, too."

She folded her arms across her chest, stared at the road. They were staying off the interstate, taking local roads. Wherever they were going, it would take longer, but Bitsy guessed it was safer.

"You know where you're going?"

He shot her a look. "The first-aid kit is on the floor. Ice your hamstring and wrap it with the elastic bandage in there. Then you should get some sleep."

She picked up the first-aid kit. "When are you going to sleep?"

"Don't worry about me."

"You have any family?" She unwrapped the makeshift bandage from her leg.

Mick glanced at her thigh. The swelling looked the same but the skin had discolored. "No."

"Guess it's hard to have a normal life in your kind of business." She took the disposable ice pack from the first-aid kit, squeezing it until its inner pouch ruptured and the cold ice set. She applied the bag, giving a start as the cold met her tender flesh.

He drove.

"Secret identities and undercover work and all that spy stuff... Bet it's exciting. Never a dull moment."

He looked at the digital clock on the dashboard as if calculating how much longer she could last before exhaustion overwhelmed her.

"I used to crave the wild side myself. The more excitement, the better. Late nights, bad boys, living on the edge. That was me." She shifted the ice pack. "That's how I met my husband. Ex-husband."

Mick rubbed his face as if weary.

"You are tired," she accused.

"We both could use some sleep," he said. "As soon as I find a spot that's safe, I'll pull over. Safer to travel after dark anyway. I would have stayed at the motel but there was always the possibility they tracked down the BMW and would force Smiley to answer some questions."

"If we had stayed on the coast, I know a place we could have gone."

He looked at her skeptically.

"I do. A friend of mine has a cabin up north. Very

secluded. He uses it for weekend getaways or sometimes for his high-profile clients who need a place to get away from the media."

Mick's expression stayed skeptical. "What kind of clients does your friend have?"

"Generally wives divorcing or being divorced by their rich, powerful husbands and unwilling to abandon the lifestyle they have become accustomed to. Or they just plain want to stick it to the son of a bitch."

"Is that what you did? Stuck it to the son of a bitch?"

"No, I just wanted out as quickly and painlessly as possible."

"Was it? Quick and painless?"

"Not for one minute." Without pausing to reflect, she said, "My friend Grey handled my divorce, but I didn't go for the big bucks. He tried to keep it out of the media, too. He wasn't as successful there."

"Why?"

"I was married to Johnny Dumont. Of Dumont Multi-Media."

Mick gave a low whistle.

"You've heard of him?"

"I know the conglomerate. I can see why your divorce was hard to keep out of the public eye."

"Every competitor they have wanted a piece of it. Of course, Dumont Multi-Media's coverage was slightly more biased. They had me all but seducing the family Great Dane by the time they finished with me."

Mick smiled. "Sorry. I know it's not funny."

Bitsy shrugged away his apology and smiled herself. "You didn't read the stories."

"No, but I can imagine a guy like that, all that power, all that money. He was probably used to doing whatever he wanted."

He'd caught her off guard, understanding like that.

"I've seen a lot of guys like that. Sometimes they fall. Sometimes nothing touches them."

"Is that your job? To make them fall?"

He shrugged. "I was one small man in a big organization. I'd get my assignment, do it and hope it contributed somehow to the greater good."

"What about now? Do you think everything your organization did was for the greater good?"

"I had to, if I was going to do my job. But I was never a fool. It's an organization of humans and humans have flaws."

"Maybe but only some are murderers." They drove in silence until Bitsy said, "You know what I hate him the most for?"

Mick glanced at her.

"He took away my illusions. The white knight, endless love, two halves of a whole. I really fell for that crapola. Hell, as long as I can remember, that's all I wanted. A man I loved unconditionally and who loved me back unconditionally. Children. A family."

Mick shrugged. "That's not impossible. Look around you. Lots of people have that."

"You don't."

"I'm not lots of people."

Bitsy smiled. "That's for sure." She waved her hand as if pushing the subject away. "Anyway, I don't believe in happily-ever-after anymore. Marriage to Johnny took that from me. That's what I regret the most."

"So, that's why you're hiding out in the morgue? Some dude broke your heart?"

"It's not a morgue. It's a mortuary. And I'm not hiding. I'm…" She searched for the right term. "I'm reevaluating."

"Come off it. You're shaking in your boots. You know how many hearts get broken every day?"

"How many have you broken?"

"None intentionally."

She made a h-m-m-rumph noise.

"Everyone gets their heart broken. It's part of life."

"How many times has your heart been broken?"

He kept his gaze steady on the road. He didn't answer. His eyes had a far-off look as if he saw something else. Someone else. "Once."

"Your wife?" Bitsy said softly. She did not expect a response. For several seconds, she did not get it, then he spoke in a strange, distant tone.

"We were young. We fell in love. And then she was pregnant. And there it was—a wife, a child, a family. She was getting into a car. I opened the door for her and was holding it. She was almost inside when she turned to press herself to me and give me a kiss. I could feel the small swell of her belly. Then her body jerked. The bullet hit her square in the back of her head. No sound. A silencer was used. I was standing there, bits of brain and blood on me. The wife, the child, the family was gone."

"Who shot her?"

"A hired professional."

"Did you ever learn his identity?"

"I knew it before she was buried."

"What did you do?"

"I went undercover. Eventually I put him and the two out of three men who operated the central Midwest territories in jail."

"What happened to the third?"

"He was lucky. He had a heart attack. Massive."

"Why did they shoot your wife?"

"The bullet was meant for me."

The words hung in the air. To anyone else, she would say she was sorry but this hard-featured man beside her did not want her sympathy.

"Why did they want to kill you?"

"I had once worked for them. When I met Lisa, I decided to get out, start a new life, make a clean break. Problem was, I knew where the bodies were buried, in a manner of speaking. I never did any of the dirty work, but I knew how the operation was run. What they didn't know was that I'd have taken it to my grave, if they hadn't tried to put me there prematurely."

When the pop sounded outside the car, Bitsy's first thought was firecrackers, the kind strung together that once ignited, erupted into a series of explosions on a Fourth of July night. Lanie had a shitzu so terrified of the noise, the dog spent the entire Independence Day holiday weekend zoned out on dog tranquilizers.

Another bang-bang had Bitsy thinking the dog had the right idea when the car swerved and weaved wildly all over the road.

Mick swore. "They got a tire."

"Who got a what?" Bitsy looked over her shoulder to see what Mick was watching so intently in the rearview mirror. She saw a nondescript van, heard another series of firecracker pops. Her curse rivaled Mick's. "They found us?"

"I don't think they're shooting for sport. They must have been tracking Smiley." Mick maneuvered the car into the other lane. Bitsy saw the speedometer needle climb toward eighty.

"What the—"

She was interrupted as the back windshield exploded. Pebbles of shatterproof glass ricocheted through the car. Bitsy ducked to the seat, one shard catching her in the neck. She cried out from the sharp sting.

"Are you hit?" Mick's hand covered hers pressed to her neck. "Let me see. Are you bleeding?"

"I'm okay. It was a piece of the windshield." She raised her head far enough to see a pickup heading straight at them.

"Mick," she yelled, reaching for the wheel. He

slapped her hand away hard, jerking the wheel sharply to the left at the same time. "Hang on."

The car tipped sideways as they climbed onto the road's banked side. She heard tires screeching, brakes shrieking. She squeezed her eyes shut, tensing her body, waiting to hear the crash of metal meeting metal. Instead she heard Mick curse. "That will only slow them down."

She popped her head up, saw the van chasing them coming out of a spin, its front end pointed away from their own speeding vehicle. Mick rounded a curve on two wheels, throwing her against the side, and the van was no longer in sight. Mick kept the gas pedal pressed to the floor. They shot forward. Bitsy righted herself and sat up, rubbing her shoulder. Her neck still smarted where it had been hit by the glass, and a wide red mark crossed her wrist where Mick had slapped her hand.

"See that sharp turn there?" Mick yelled above the wind howling in through the back windshield. "On the count of three, open your door and jump. Tuck your head and feet and roll."

Bitsy stared at him, certain the rushing air had distorted his words. "Did you say—"

"One…"

"Jump? Jump out of a car going…" She glanced at the speedometer. The needle moved toward eighty-five.

"Two…"

"Eighty-freakin'-five miles an hour?"

They were almost at the curve, which sheared off into a drop of over a thousand feet into an open field below. Mick pointed the car straight at the curve.

"Three. Now, now, now," Mick ordered, grabbing the door handle, pushing open the door and hurling himself out of the car. Screaming, Bitsy followed his lead, hitting the ground with a bone-shattering thud, then rolling across hard concrete and finally landing hard on her side, the impact stunning her so that for a moment she could only lie huddled, aware of her heart thudding against her chest. Dazed, she watched the hatchback sail Thelma-and-Louise style over the drop-off, then disappear. Her body flinched as the crash sounded, but before she had time to think, Mick was at her side, pulling her up by her arm, almost wrenching it out of its socket. The car exploded, a flash of hot light from below.

"Come on. Let's go." He dragged her up the embankment into the woods that lined the other side of the road. "They'll be rounding that corner in another second." She scrambled up the rise in her heelless shoes, any pain from her hamstring injury superceded by sheer terror.

"It will take them a little time to figure out there's not two charred bodies in there, but not much."

As soon as they made it to the cover of the woods, Bitsy halted, bent double, breathing hard. Past the trees on the roadway below, brakes squealed to a stop.

"Come on." Doors slammed.

"I don't know how many of them there are, but they'll probably send in a few to check the woods."

A siren sounded far off. They were deep in the woods now. Her leg screamed with pain. She straightened, ignoring it, and took a step. When she stumbled. Mick caught her in his arms. She clung to his chest and cursed, frustration filling her.

"Here." Disentangling her hands from his shirt, Mick turned his back to her and crouched, looking up at her from the side. "Jump on."

"Huh?"

"Jump on," he ordered through gritted teeth, "before they kill us both."

The reminder of death's possibility looming too close for comfort roused Bitsy. She leaped onto his back, wrapping her arms around his neck and locking her legs around his middle.

They started off at a slow gallop, the sounds of emergency vehicles filling the air behind them. The woods were dense. They had only gone a short distance when they heard the sound of men's voices in the distance.

"Mick?" Bitsy whispered close to his ear. "What do we do now?"

"Good question."

"I have an idea."

Chapter Eight

From above, Bitsy watched the two men running through the forest. With Mick's help, she had swung up onto a low but sturdy branch, then climbed several higher ones, ignoring the pain in her leg, until she was halfway up the sturdy oak. She perched about a hundred feet above, wedged in the V of a branch and tree trunk, and felt invincible. Grey would have been proud.

Two trees over, Mick sat ten feet higher in similar fashion in an equally sturdy black maple, his gaze zeroed in on the two men moving below them.

From her vantage point, Bitsy could see the van parked on the side of the road. A police cruiser had pulled up behind it. An officer had gotten out and walked over to the van's driver and was interviewing him. A few minutes later, the officer flipped closed his notepad and stood beside the driver, facing the drop-off, watching the action below. When the officer said something, the man nodded. The officer walked back to the cruiser, got inside and pulled away. The driver glanced back at the woods, then leaned against the van's front end, lit a cigarette and kept an eye on the crash scene.

The two men in the woods had separated and gone in opposite directions. They each held a gun in one hand and a slim silver box in the other that they spoke into periodically. They didn't look like hoods. They were lean and slick in dark clothing and mirrored aviator-style sunglasses that concealed their eyes. Government issue. She thought of Mick perched above her. He did not look government like the men below, nor gangster like the animal who had attempted to rearrange her face this morning. But beyond his harsh handsomeness, Mick had the air of a neighborhood boy whose front teeth had been punched out before he was ten.

The men were in sight but moving deeper into the wilderness. Their run had slowed to a loping jog as they moved one way, then angled another, then back again, like a cornered rabbit trying to outwit its opponent. One spoke into the silver walkie-talkie, then the other one. Their pace became a walk, and after a few more minutes, they turned around back to the highway.

Bitsy glanced up at Mick as the men moved out of the woods toward the van. He shook his head. She had no intention of moving, nor did her body. Her muscles ached, newly bruised by the tuck-and-roll from the car. Fortunately nothing had been broken.

Her limbs felt heavy from physical battering and fatigue, but the weight was off her leg, and the pain had dimmed to a mean but manageable throb. Memories of her childhood tree climbs came back to her. She felt now as she had then. High above the world, everything at a distance, she felt safe. She had not felt that way in a long time, and she was grateful for the respite. Soon they would be back on solid ground and running, or at least, for her, limping for their lives.

The men formed a semicircle in front of the van. They had tucked their guns, crossed their arms, their expressions stoic as they studied the scene below. They spoke without looking at each other. Occasionally a head turned to scan the area. One of the men from the woods pointed beyond the drop-off to a ridge where the woods sloped and opened onto the highway below. He drew a wide arc with his index finger. The others listened, expressionless, then both the men who had been in the woods turned toward the driver as if waiting for a decision. Bitsy saw his thin lips barely move. All three men turned and climbed into the van. The vehicle pulled away, heading east.

Bitsy looked up, light-headed with temporary victory. She smiled a wide, toothy grin, sat high in her tree and did not want to leave. Mick looked at her, not returning her smile. Instead he signaled her to climb down and lowered himself to the next branch. She reluctantly did the same, careful to keep her weight on her good leg. Mick was on the ground below her when she reached the bottom branch. He raised his arms and she eased herself down into his embrace. For a second, he held her there suspended. Then he set her feet to the ground and his hands released her.

"They either went down to the scene to see if they could find out anything, or they're circling back around, hoping to catch us if we come out the other side of the woods."

He crouched down and pulled out a cell phone he had slipped inside his sneaker beneath the laces and padded tongue. "I can't get a signal." He snapped it closed and stuck it into his pants' pocket. "For now, we'll head northeast, deeper into the woods. The farther away from civilization, the safer. Especially if our little search party decides to try again. There are trails and campgrounds all over this area. Eventually we'll run into something." His gaze dropped to Bitsy's leg. "The only problem is, we'll have to go it on foot."

Bitsy straightened, feeling brave and still slightly giddy from their latest escape. "I can walk."

"And I can fly."

"I can walk," Bitsy insisted. "At least a little way, if we don't go too fast," she qualified.

"Show me."

She pressed her lips together and took several sturdy steps, ignoring the pain that made her knee want to buckle.

Mick watched her, his head tilted to one side. "You're faking it, but I'm impressed."

"Is that so?" She took several more defiant steps. It was far from a saunter but she was still standing. She turned to face him.

"After a half hour, you'll be dead on your feet and they'll have apprehended us." He sighed, turned his back to her and crouched. "Hop on. I can carry you."

"I can walk."

"Lady, this isn't a sack race. It's a race…"

Bitsy looked at him as his voice trailed off. He straightened, smiling slowly, his eyes brightening. She could almost see the lightbulb going off.

"What?" She was almost afraid to ask.

"Two heads are better than one." He squatted down, unwrapping the elastic bandages from the first-aid kit that she'd tied around her thigh and knee for support. "And three legs are better than two."

He lined himself up beside her and, using the bandages, began to wrap his leg to hers.

"Wait a minute."

"We've already waited too many minutes. Those men could be back any minute, and we'll still be standing here, arguing like an old married couple." He finished tethering their legs together and fastened the ends securely. "Lean against me. Wrap your arm around my waist. I'll support your weight to keep most of it off your left leg. Let's try it. Wrap your arm around my waist."

She looked at him, her lips pursed. He draped his own arm around her shoulders.

"C'mon, don't be shy." He smiled.

With a dry look, she slapped her arm around his waist. When he pulled her tight to his side, she became acutely aware of cords of toned abdominal muscles. He was at least five inches taller than her so that she nestled perfectly under his armpit.

"Ow. Damn gun's poking me in the side."

"Let me go and I'll stick it on the other side."

His arm fell away from her shoulders and she released his waist. He peeled the T-shirt up over his head. She didn't even attempt to avert her gaze from the man's bare, broad shoulders, wide chest, rippled stomach that narrowed into slim, strong hips. Lord knew how much longer she had to live. Now wasn't the time not to appreciate any of life's little bonuses. He switched the gun holster to the other side. As he hunched his shoulders to pull the T-shirt back on, she saw bruises from his hurtle from the car darkening the skin along his upper back. What she'd feared all along was true. The man was flesh and blood.

His head popped through the shirt's neck opening and he wiggled into the rest of it, smoothed it down his torso. Bitsy suppressed a sigh.

He draped his arm along her shoulders again and drew her to his side. "Okay, let's try this. We'll lead with our outer feet on the count of three. One…"

She snaked her arm around his narrow waist, her fingers splayed on his rib cage. "You like that one-two-three bit, don't you?" she snapped, but she let him pull her closer to his side.

"Two…"

She wrinkled her nose. "When's the last time you showered?"

"Probably about the last time you did, rosebud. Enough chitchat. Let's go." They moved forward awkwardly.

"Lean into me. Let me support you. Stick your foot on top of mine if it helps. That's it."

"Stop telling me what to do."

At first, their progress was slow and ungainly, but after a few steps, Mick learned to adjust his step to meet her own shortened gait. She mastered the rhythm of shifting her weight so either Mick or her outer leg bore the bulk of it. They matched their pace and, although their strides were shortened, their speed compensated.

Bitsy laughed. "It's working. It's really working."

Mick looked down at her, amused. "In a manner of speaking. At least it should get us somewhere until we can find a better mode of transportation. Which hopefully won't be long."

They moved into the thick of the woods, all sounds of traffic and civilization gradually fading. Eventually they were left with only the sounds of the birds and the wind and the sensation of being entirely alone. Mick slowed his steps even further to meet hers. She added a hop at the end of hers to lengthen her stride.

"Did you recognize the men in the van?" she asked him.

"They were on my team for the arms raid," he said in a tight voice. "Careful." His body pulled her up as they came to a jutting tree root. Her weight involuntarily pressed into his side as his arm tightened around her shoulders. Once they'd stepped over the high root, his grasp eased.

"Were they just following orders?" Bitterness edged her words.

"Yes. And they wouldn't have hesitated to kill us both if necessary."

"Do you think they are in on the setup? Or do they really believe you're a rogue agent who tried to assassinate a congressman?"

"It doesn't matter what they believe. They were given the assignment. They don't ask for a reason. They carry it out. A botched operation, an agent on the loose who was supposed to be silenced. The entire organization is at risk. They won't stop until it's secure again. To enlist their aid, law enforcement outside the Agency will be told I'm an assassin. But inside the Agency, I'm a threat now."

"Why you?"

"Either I came too close to something someone prefers not to have uncovered or someone needed a fall guy. Either way, the order came down and I was the jackpot winner. Whoever issued the order is someone outside the organization. Taking out an operative could come from the inside, but a congressman? Whoever wanted to get rid of two birds with one stone is someone big."

"Except both birds are still alive," Bitsy noted.

They trudged forward, the woods endless and dizzying and isolated. The sounds of nature and the sense of being within a secret world had long stopped being soothing, but they also didn't hear the sounds of their pursuers.

It had been several hours since they'd last eaten and much longer since either had slept. Bitsy's body felt battered and sore. Her face was swollen, her leg ached. Her head hurt, and her spirit was deflating along with her optimism.

"Did you take the pill I gave you?"

"No."

A quick smile lit his face. "I didn't think you would."

"What time do you think it is?" she asked.

Mick looked through the treetops to the semi-visible sun. "Around 4:00 p.m."

"We need to find something before dark, right?"

"We will."

"How can you be so sure?"

He glanced at her. "It beats being afraid."

"I'm not afraid."

"Good."

They walked their three-legged gait a few more steps.

"Are you telling me you're not even a little bit afraid?"

"Only a fool wouldn't be afraid." Mick smiled

that devastating smile at her that still made her blush inside. "Only a bigger fool would admit it."

They walked another half mile before they reached a narrow road, not much wider than a trail, probably one of the old logging roads. Mick stopped, pulling Bitsy up short beside him.

"It's got to lead somewhere," he said.

"Yeah, deeper into the woods," Bitsy said.

Still, the rough road was easier to navigate than the untamed forest with its tangle of tree roots, high grasses and scratchy bushes. Fatigue, physical and mental, had overtaken Bitsy. She thought no further than putting one foot in front of the other, her entire existence reduced to a series of steps supported by the man at her side.

"I don't suppose you were a Boy Scout, were you, Mick?"

"What do you think?"

"I think you're out of your element."

He gave her a dry once-over. "And you're not?"

"I was a Camp Fire girl."

"Whoopee for you. Got any survival tips you'd like to share?"

He took a longer stride than usual. She double hopped to keep up. "Yeah, stay away from men with guns strapped to their sides."

He smiled. "What about men with a woman who won't shut up strapped to their sides?"

The trail rose, then leveled, revealing an open canyon below. On the other side was a sign that announced Haile's Hole, a campground complete with camping, fishing, and boating, according to its on-site advertising. Mick and Bitsy both stopped when they saw the sign. Mick turned and looked Bitsy over from top to bottom.

"You look like crap. How bad do I look?"

She examined the man beside her. The red rings around his eyes from the hair spray had lessened. His hair was the type that, even mussed up, looked adorable. His ill-fitting clothes gave him the look of the Hulk. He was dirty, smelly and unshaven. She knew she looked worse.

"Like the village idiot."

"Then I look exactly how I feel."

"What about me?"

He gave her another long examination. She did not need a mirror to imagine the swollen mouth, the bruised lower half of her face. She could see for herself the streaks of dirt on her clothes and body.

He smiled. "Like you were rode hard and put away wet."

"That good, huh? Quit grinning. It only adds to the village-idiot image."

He looked over at the campgrounds. A vehicle was in the lot. A pickup truck was parked farther back by a utilities building. "It's not prime season. Doesn't look like much activity, but there's some staff. Probably still have reservations for the week-ends, and during the week, they use the down time for maintenance. We'll say we swerved to avoid an animal, overcorrected and the car crashed into a tree," he thought aloud. "That will explain the bruises. You were driving. That will explain the accident." He grinned wickedly.

She pursed her lips, gestured to their clothes. "What about our haute couture?"

"We were on our way home from a wild Halloween party and decided to take a little romantic detour up into the mountains to watch the sunrise. We both fell asleep, lost our way and, well, you know the rest."

She considered the story. "I guess it's more believable than I was kidnapped by a corpse."

"I'll offer them money to use the phone, maybe see if one of them can give us a ride to the nearest town."

"Beats battling goons."

He grabbed her by the shoulders, startling her. His fingers were forceful but not painful on her flesh. "If you so much as breathe wrong, not only will you put your life at risk, but the lives of other innocent people, too. Understood?"

She didn't believe he would shoot her, or innocent people. On the other hand, she wasn't about to call his bluff.

She tried to jerk away from his grip, but he held her firm. "And what do you think I am? The criminal mastermind behind this mess?" she asked.

He ignored her question. "Do you understand?" he repeated.

"Understood."

"Good." He released her, and she twisted away from him. He bent down and unfastened the bandages that wrapped their limbs together. "I'll help you down and carry you in my arms when we get closer. It will add the heroic touch."

"Yeah, women will be falling at your feet."

Mick wadded up the bandages. "C'mon, darling, let's go."

She had no choice but to lean on him as they made their way down the slope to the campgrounds. They cut through a children's play area, where Mick chucked the bandages into a trash can, then swept Bitsy into his arms and carried her the last one hundred feet.

"Look over there," she said. Longing swelled her voice. Mick looked in the direction of her pointed finger and saw the object of her desire. A concrete-block building. On its side, painted in bright blue stenciled letters was Bath House.

"First girl I've ever seen go giddy over the idea of toilet paper," Mick mumbled.

"And running water," Bitsy added, her gaze still riveted on the flat-roofed building. Her hair felt limp; her body was rank. She wouldn't sell her soul for a shower, but she was open to negotiations.

Mick stopped before a sprawling log cabin with a railed front porch. A large sign in the window outside said Office. Check In On Arrival. He carried her up the stairs, opened the screened door and let it slam behind them.

A heavyset woman in her mid-forties with a cap of gray hair and an earthy appearance came out of a room in back of an area separated by a counter that held a variety of brochures. "Lloyd, I'm heading—"

She stopped when she saw it wasn't Lloyd. She eagle-eyed the couple as Mick approached the check-in area with Bitsy in his arms.

"This ain't no honeymoon hotel," she said. "Plus we're shut down this week for maintenance. No rentals available." She surveyed them once more, her eyes narrowing on Bitsy's bruised face. "Although you two don't look like you're here for vacation."

Mick eased Bitsy down until her feet touched the floor. She stood, but leaned against him for effect. He draped his arm around her shoulders.

"No, ma'am." Mick adopted an aw-shucks accent. "Vacation is not exactly what we'd call the last twelve hours."

With a keen gaze, the woman waited for him to go on.

"See, my little pumpkin, Ethel, and I..." Mick elbowed Bitsy in the ribs. She smiled at the woman like a trained monkey and gave a little curtsy. "We were at a friend's Halloween party last night and decided we'd take a little ride up into the high grounds." He squeezed Bitsy, pulling her tighter to him. She sent him an adoring glance, shot him another smile.

"And we got lost."

"Shouldn't drive when you been drinking," the woman said, tight-lipped.

"Oh, I don't drink," Bitsy interjected.

"That's why she was driving," Mick added. "And had the accident."

"Accident?" the woman echoed.

"I saw a goat."

"A goat?" the woman questioned.

"It was a woodchuck, honey bunch." In an aside to the woman, Mick noted, "She's a city girl."

"It was a goat," Bitsy insisted. "A mountain goat."

"Sure, dear, whatever you say." Turning slightly away from her, he rolled his eyes at the woman. The woman's suspicious expression softened.

"Don't patronize me, sweet cheeks," Bitsy said through gritted teeth.

"Okay, folks, let's just say you saw an animal. Up here in these parts in the dark, it could have been Bigfoot, for all we know."

"It was a goat," Bitsy muttered under her breath.

The woman looked at her. "Maybe you'd like to sit down?"

She was warming up to them, Bitsy thought. "Thank you, ma'am, that's very kind. We were walking, stumbling around in the dark actually, and I tripped over a tree root or something—"

"Sure, it wasn't a goat?" Mick asked dryly.

Bitsy shot him a look to kill. She looked back at the older woman, her expression exclaiming, "Men!"

The woman smiled, lifted the hinged portion of

the countertop. "Why don't you both come around into the back room. There's a couple of chairs. How about a soda?"

They'd hit pay dirt. "That'd be wonderful," Bitsy exclaimed with genuine enthusiasm.

"Cola? Root beer? Orange? I've got a few Yoohoos squirreled away, too, in the store refrigerator. Part of my secret stash."

"I adore Yoo-hoo," Mick drawled, giving the woman the direct impact of his eighty-watt smile.

"Orange sounds fabu to me." Bitsy smiled gratefully at the woman, her mouth already watering with the idea of sugar and artificial color.

"Be back in a jiff," the woman promised.

Bitsy waited until the woman's ample backside disappeared into the rear of the building before she whispered, "Do I look like an Ethel?"

"Well, what exactly does a Bitsy look like?"

"There's nothing wrong with the name Bitsy."

"For one, it rhymes with *ditzy*."

"If I wasn't such a lady, I'd tell you what Mick rhymes with."

He smiled. "Come clean. You're no lady."

She turned her head, ignoring him.

"Hey, you name me, okay?"

Bitsy swung her head back to him. "With pleasure."

They heard the woman approach and stopped talking.

"Here we go now." The woman entered, brandishing two bottles so cold, condensation had formed on the outside of the glass. Bitsy had never seen anything so beautiful in her life. She thanked the woman, raised the bottle to her lips and, gulping convulsively, swallowed half of it before pulling it away. She wiped her mouth with the back of her hand, saw the woman and Mick watching her.

"My favorite," she explained. She looked at Mick's untouched Yoo-hoo. "Drink up, Leslie."

He smiled and clinked his bottle against hers in salute.

"Leslie. Now there's a man's name you don't hear often enough nowadays. My father was named Leslie," the woman noted, beaming at Mick.

Figures, Bitsy thought.

"Mine, too," Mick said, amazed, and he and the woman both laughed. Bitsy chugged another quarter bottle of the orange soda.

"So, where were we?" Mick said.

"The accident," the woman supplied.

"Yes, Ethel June swerved to avoid whatever was in the road and then overcorrected and *bam*." Mick smacked his hands together. Bitsy and the woman both jumped. "Right into a Douglas fir."

"How horrible," the woman sympathized.

"Totaled the Porsche," Mick said with a hangdog expression.

"*My* Porsche," Bitsy added.

The woman turned her compassionate expression to her.

"There we were, lost, stuck out in the middle of

nowhere, with no idea what was going to happen," Bitsy continued.

"So, we started to walk," Mick said picking up the thread.

"And walk and walk and walk and—"

"She gets the picture, Ethel. And here we are."

The woman clucked her tongue. "You poor kids."

"Us poor kids," Bitsy echoed.

"You've been through quite an ordeal. You must be starving."

Bitsy gave the woman her best big-eyed expression.

"Lucky for you, I stuck around a little while after the workers left."

"It's a miracle," Mick said.

"Praise the Lord," Bitsy added.

"All right, then." The woman clapped her hands purposefully as she stood. "We need to get you back to civilization."

Mick said, "If there's a town nearby where you can drop us or we can make a call and have someone come and pick us up—"

"Nonsense. I have a house in town about thirty minutes south of here. Let me just shut down the computer, get my things together and I'll take you home. You can call somebody from there and get cleaned up and have a good meal while you're waiting."

Bitsy looked at Mick. "We don't want to put you to any trouble, ma'am. You can just drop us off somewhere and we'll wait for a ride."

"Don't you fret none." The woman walked behind the desk to the computer and moved the mouse on the pad. "It will be nice—" She paused, frowned at the screen. She glanced at her two guests, then back at the screen.

"Something wrong?" Mick asked.

The woman looked up, preoccupied. "No, no. I'm still learning the silly thing, that's all." She looked again at the screen, clicked the mouse. "There we go. Where were we? Oh, yes, you're coming home with me. I just need to grab a few things I left in the storage room and we'll be on our way." She waddled away.

"I'd ease up on the charm, Deuce Bigalow," Bitsy whispered to Mick once the woman was out of sight.

Mick sidled a glance at her. "You admit I have charm?"

"You don't have to make her fall in love with you."

"It's a curse."

"I'll admit I'm all for getting cleaned up and eating a good meal, but it would have been easier to have her drop us somewhere."

"Why?"

"She'll be expecting someone to pick us up."

"Someone will."

"Who? Another one of your comrades?"

"You're rather young to be so cynical."

"You're never too young to be cynical."

Mick didn't argue. He was older than her in more

than years. He did say, "*Your* Porsche, Ethel?" He cocked an eyebrow at her.

She was about to answer when they heard a car engine. Mick jumped to his feet and moved toward the front door. Bitsy followed as fast as her throbbing leg would let her. She joined Mick at the window just in time to see the red taillights and their saving angel disappear.

Chapter Nine

"Where's she going?" Bitsy asked, staring at the spot where the taillights had vanished as if her will alone could make them and the woman reappear.

"Something spooked her." Mick turned and scanned the room.

"What?"

Not answering, he headed toward the office, rounded the maple desk and sat down in front of the computer. Bitsy followed him into the narrow room and stood behind him as he switched on the machine.

"She saw something on the computer?" Bitsy wondered. "We're not on the Net, are we?"

"Everybody's on the Net. Greatest spy device ever invented." Mick clicked on the Internet browser icon. A home page filled the screen. It was a celebrity site of star gossip detailing who was doing what with whom and where.

Leaning over Mick's shoulder, Bitsy scanned the page. There, in the lower right-hand corner, under the screaming headlines and paparazzi photos, she saw herself.

"What the—?" She leaned in closer. The white lab coat she wore was open, revealing her Halloween costume. Her heavily made-up face was in profile, partially hidden by her sky high hairstyle, as she was led into Canaan's satellite police station. Beside the photo was a smaller pencil sketch of a man's face that vaguely resembled Mick.

"God, I look like a hooker."

"Fishnets and leather tend to have that effect."

Bitsy leaned in even closer to read the caption under the photo. "'Ex-gold digger turns to crime.' Ex-gold digger!"

A bold-faced link said, "For complete story, click here." Mick clicked.

The home page dissolved and another picture of Bitsy came onto the screen, even larger and more lifelike. The full-length frontal shot showed Bitsy in her vampire vixen costume, looking even taller in her spiked heels beside the short, older cop holding her arm. A Canaan police cruiser was clearly in the background.

Mick read, "'Ex-wife of Johnny Dumont, heir to Dumont Multi-Media Industries, has been forced to turn to other means to make ends meet.'" Mick sat back. "Married to all those billions."

"Your point?" Bitsy demanded, tight-lipped.

Mick shook his head. "And now you're a hooker."

"I am not a— Is that what it says?" She scanned the page.

"You know what they say. A picture is worth a thousand words." He smiled and continued reading, "'Bitsy Leigh, former wife of Johnny Dumont, heir apparent to industry giant Dumont Multi-Media, was brought in to the Canaan Town Police Station last night in connection with her possible involvement with a man suspected in the assassination plot of Congressman Radley Kittredge'" Mick stopped grinning.

"It's worse than I thought," Bitsy said.

Mick read on. "Police would neither confirm nor deny if Leigh was romantically involved with the suspect, Michael James. Leigh's cousin, Lanie Morrison, of 32 Hillock Lane, reported she had seen Leigh early the next morning with a man fitting the suspect's description. Morrison has not been able to contact her cousin since that time. However, Morrison insisted the only crime committed is even the innuendo that her cousin would voluntarily and willingly consort with an alleged assassin. Morrison stated, 'There obviously is a perfectly good rationale for this entire misunderstanding, and I have no doubt my cousin will supply it.' Morrison noted she had filed a missing-persons report with the California Department of Justice. In the meantime, she asked anyone with information on her cousin to please contact her or police."

"Poor Lanie. She must be out of her mind with worry. I've got to call her." Bitsy reached for the phone beside the computer. Mick grabbed her wrist. She glared at him.

"She's already too vulnerable. I told you before if they know they can get to you through her, they will."

"Who's 'they'? The good guys or the bad guys?"

"You must have learned by now that there's a fine line between those two camps. And both want to win at any cost."

"So you're saying my cousin's life is in danger now, too?"

"No, but the more you involve her, the greater the risk to her. If you call her, they'll know. If you send her an e-mail, they'll know. The more technology becomes part of the average Joe's daily life, the easier it's become for Big Brother. Computers, phones, mail, the Agency can track it all, but in this day of satellite scanners and digital technology, anything on the airwaves can be tapped into and it usually requires no more than a scan and the push of a button. There have been twelve-year-olds who've done it as if it were the latest video game. If you contact your cousin, they'll know, and they'll use it to their advantage."

Bitsy stared at the computer screen. "How come they couldn't come up with any pictures of you except a lousy artist's sketch?"

"I avoid having photos taking of me. Makes it slightly difficult for me to remain incognito. Also, Arthur, the man who was killed, destroyed my identity. I don't exist."

"Of course." Bitsy sighed.

Mick clicked the computer to a search program, then typed in her name. Hits from Web sites across the country and internationally filled the screen. Mick clicked randomly. They saw the same photo and similar story several times.

"Some stringer could have been hanging around, looking for a story," Mick suggested. "Not a bad angle. 'Halloween in the City of Death.' He could have heard the call go out over the scanner and caught them bringing you in. The photo would have gone out on the wire and been picked up nationally. More likely though the story was planted by the Agency. Either way, our friend here saw these pictures when she went to turn off the computer and recognized us." He stood. "We don't have much time before she alerts the local boys. We've got to get out of here. Check in the other rooms for food, blankets, anything we could use. I'll be outside." He winked at her encouragingly. "Making transportation arrangements."

She went toward the back of the building as Mick headed out the front door. As she rounded a walled partition, she stopped and smiled. Spread out before her was a small store selling a variety of supplies for the campground's residents. There were shelves of bug repellant, bandages, flashlights, batteries, matches, candles and ropes, but no items so coveted as the shelves of food and drink spreading before Bitsy like a bacchanalian feast.

She picked up an overpriced can of cashews, popped open the lid, and, not even trying to be delicate, threw a handful in her mouth and chewed contentedly. She grabbed another handful and, cheeks bulging like a supermodel gone wild, she ripped several plastic bags from the stack hanging on the side of the cash-register counter and began to fill them. She took two coolers off the top of a stack on the floor and headed to the fridges. They had passed a padlocked freezer advertising ice $1 a Bag in the front of the building. If they had time, she would look for the key. If not, the coolers would keep the items inside them cold for several hours. As she slid back the glass door of the first fridge, she heard a knock. She froze. The knock came again, more insistent, then it became a pounding. She crept to the end of an aisle and, crouching down, peeked around it in the direction of the pounding. With relief, she saw Mick through the attached small back room's door window.

She went to the door and unlocked it. Throwing it back, she gestured with a flourish to the room behind them. "Look at this place. As God is my witness," she said in a cheesy drawl, "I'll never be hungry again."

He looked at her as if she were a few slices short of a full loaf. "What took you so long?" He strode past her into the store. "I need a hacksaw and a piece of wire."

"Bet you chew nails, too."

He shook his head, plucking a wire coat hanger from a row of coat hooks on the wall and slipped the sweater off its frame. "You amuse yourself, don't you?"

"I have a certain *je ne sais quoi.*"

He smiled as he untwisted the hanger, straightened it into one long length and bent one end into a fish hook.

"You're certainly in a good mood for a prostitute fugitive."

"Food tends to do it for me." She thrust the open can of cashews at him. "Have some and all your problems will disappear."

He stuck his hand into the can, his gaze assessing her. "When's the last time you slept?"

"Flip-flops!" Ignoring him, Bitsy made a beeline toward a plastic bucket of rubber foot thongs in a variety of colors. She slipped off her modified heels and tried on a yellow pair, turning her foot admiringly. Past the bucket in a small arched alcove were shelves stacked with T-shirts and hooded sweatshirts, gym shorts and nylon pants. Bitsy picked up a sky-blue T-shirt. Printed across its front was *I Camp in a Haile Hole.* Off to the side, in an end-aisle display, she saw the toothbrushes and mouthwash and soap. How could she have overlooked toiletries?

Mick had headed out the back door, armed with a modified wire hanger and a slim saw he had found Lord knew where. Bitsy had been too busy stocking up on supplies. She carried the bulging sacks to the back door to set them on the narrow platform porch.

Mick moved to the pickup truck they had spotted earlier, probably used by staff to run errands and bring in supplies. He slipped the wire hanger inside the driver's door panel. He wiggled it back and forth a few seconds and pulled upward. He opened the door and slid inside with the saw. Bitsy went back inside to get the other bags. She left the heavier coolers for Mick. When she had finished, she found a pair of ladies' nylon pants and a T shirt and went into the office, closing the door behind her. She stripped to her undergarments and pulled on the new attire. She stuffed her old clothes in a plastic sack, grabbed a sweatshirt and went out to the back porch. There she saw Mick carrying groceries and other items to the truck idling with a low purr.

"There are two coolers inside," she told him. "And men's clothes."

"Ladies', too, I see."

She shrugged. "It's no vampire-vixen costume."

"I still miss the fishnets," he said as he moved past her inside. She followed him.

"The coolers are there. The clothing's around the corner. I changed in the office."

He did the same, coming out in a proper-fitting T-shirt, track pants and flip-flops. He stopped at the counter, where he tucked a half-dozen twenties under a corner of the cash register. "Are we ready?" he asked.

"One more necessity." Bitsy noted as she moved toward a door marked Employees Only and as she suspected, found behind it a restroom.

After they both had used the facilities, Mack stacked the coolers on top of each other and picked them up. After Bitsy got the door for him, and he carried them out and he set them in the truck bed beside the other supplies. He lifted the top of one, took out a canned soda. "Want one?"

She nodded and took the soda and the open can of cashews and hopped into the front cab. As he climbed in, she offered him the snack.

"How did you get this started?" she asked, referring to their new ride.

"Sawed through the steering wheel column to release the security lock and crossed the wires to hotwire the ignition." He took a handful of nuts, dropped several into his mouth, then shifted into first gear and headed out of the campground. "I figure we have at minimum a fifteen-minute head start before they get up here and see the truck is gone. It's not much, but at least it's something."

Bitsy looked longingly at the bath house as they passed the concrete structure. She popped a consoling cashew in her mouth.

Mick headed west instead of east, back the way they had come, staying on the rural roads. "You're going back toward the coast?" Bitsy asked.

"We'll cut up north and cross back later. For now, everybody expects us to run away. No one expects us to run to them. By the time they suspect we might have passed them, all they'll remember is our taillights."

Darkness fell, made even deeper by desolated back roads and the forest's thick cover. Bitsy's head started to nod as they moved out of the wooded mountains. By the time Mick cut north on forty-nine, she was snoring lightly, her left hand still curled around the can in her lap. He reached over and slipped it out of her grip. She shifted, rearranging her body against the side of the seat. She rested her cheek on her hands, her palms pressed together prayer-like. Her breathing was low and even. His discipline allowed him to resist brushing away the stray hairs that fell across her cheek. Her face, despite the bruising and swelling and smeared makeup, was as beautiful as Mick had first thought. Her expression, though, for the first time since he had met her, was peaceful. Guilt gnawed inside him as he turned away.

He did not stay long on forty-nine, turning off onto the local routes, careful not to climb too far above the speed limit despite the road's long, empty stretches. In the darkness and the silence broken only by the hum of the truck and the rhythmic breaths of the woman beside him, he thought, as he always did, of Lisa. His wife had been an enthusiastic Cubs fan, and he often liked to remember her cheering in the stands, a blue baseball cap with a red *C* on her head, her arms pumping with victory during a long base hit. He had once dreamed of her that way, except the red *C* had begun to melt, liquefying, dripping blood red down his wife's joy-filled face, and he had awoken, bathed in sweat.

That had been a long time ago, a few years after her murder. He wasn't sure exactly when the pain had stopped being sharp, like barbed wire wrapped around his heart, and had turned into an emptiness. No feeling. A void. That, he knew, was worse. Even sorrow was better than nothingness. Anything was better than nothingness. But for years and years, that was all he'd had. No fear. No happiness. No desire. No dreams.

Until he'd opened his eyes last night and seen Bitsy. He'd immediately known he was in trouble. Only now was he beginning to realize how much.

THE SOUND OF A CAR DOOR closing woke Bitsy. For a moment, she stared blankly at the man climbing into the driver's side, his profile washed red in the illumination of a neon sign. Then she remembered and sat up straight.

"Where are we?" She became instantly alert, grateful for the momentary oblivion of sleep but also frightened by the realization of her easy vulnerability. The neon light read Winnemucca Motel. The motel was laid out neatly in a long, narrow building branching off on either end to rows of rooms at nine-ty-degree angles to the main structure.

"Up north, a few miles past the Nevada border. We'll stop here for the night. " He threw a key card on the seat and turned the truck to the motel's far end. He parked and got out, rounding the cab to open Bitsy's door just as she was reaching for the handle. "Let's go."

He grabbed several sacks from the truck bed, managed to swipe the key card at the door and open it. He dropped the bags on a round table with two white plastic chairs. Dominating the small room was a queen-size bed covered in a Southwest design that matched the colors of a desert sunset print on the wall above the bed. Opposite was a small television set on the one bureau. Mick went back out for the coolers, which he set on the carpet. He grabbed a can of soda, took a long drink, then flopped down on the one armchair angled in the corner, kicked off his flipflops and stretched out. Bitsy set down tentatively on the edge of the bed.

"We're staying *here* for the night?"

"The penthouse is already booked."

"Both of us?"

He tipped back the soda can and took another drink. "Lady, I'm so tired, you could be Angelina Jolie and I'd still ask for a rain check in favor of forty."

They were reduced to the basic elements now—food, sleep, shelter…and a shower. She smiled. At this stage, sex was nowhere high up in the hierarchy of needs. She stood and went into the bathroom, where surprisingly, she found all the toiletries she'd need.

She walked out into the other room. "Do you need to use—" A deep snore cut her short. Mick's head leaned back on the chair's edge. His legs splayed out their full long length. His mouth hung open.

"Guess not," she said and padded back to the bathroom. She twisted open the shower faucets all the way. The room was already moist and blurry with steam when she peeled off her clothes and stepped into the tub. She soaped her body, and shampooed her hair and stood under the pulsing water even after the hot water ran out, the cold water invigorating. She reluctantly turned off the faucets, wrapped a towel around her body and another around her head. She brushed her teeth with the toothbrush and toothpaste and, sitting on the toilet-seat cover, combed out her hair. She wiped the steam on the mirror and inspected her face. Her nose was still bruised but the swelling had eased. Sleep, along with the shower, had helped to reduce the dark circles and puffiness beneath her eyes.

She towel dried her body, pulled back on the pants and T-shirt, but hand washed her panties and hung them to dry on the towel bar. She didn't bother with a bra. She went out into the other room where Mick remained stretched out in the chair, his snores deeper.

She rummaged through the sacks of food and took out a jar of peanut butter, a box of crackers, napkins, and a plastic knife. From the cooler, she grabbed a bottled juice and sat down at the table. She spread peanut butter on a cracker, then topped it with another one. She popped the whole cracker sandwich in her mouth and munched. She made another and another, stacking them on top of each other and washing them down with a swig of peach-guava nectar when the realization hit her. She could walk right out that door. And there was no one to stop her.

She glanced at Mick. He was still comatose. The

digital numbers on the alarm clock beside the bed changed to one-five-nine. Middle of the night. In the middle of nowhere. But she didn't know how to hotwire a vehicle. She would have to go on foot. Maybe she could go to the night manager, but she didn't want to risk involving an innocent person.

She stared at the man asleep in the chair, another realization dawning. She wasn't going anywhere. Somewhere, somehow, something had shifted, and the man stretched out, snoring loud enough to rattle the desert sunset scene off the wall, was no longer the enemy. Maybe it had happened when whoever was shooting at them earlier today had been aiming for them both. Maybe it was the fact that, instead of harming her, Mick had only kept her safe. Maybe it didn't even matter when the tide had changed. All she knew was she believed him. He would save her.

And maybe, somehow, she could save him. Before, there was only one person who wanted the real killer found. Now there were two.

She cleaned up from her snack, left on the bathroom light and the door halfway open but turned off the light in the main room and lay down on the bed. She dozed fitfully, her sleep populated by frenetic scenes of being chased, hiding in a room, crouched in a corner, someone knocking to get in.

She woke, realizing the knock on the door was no dream. Someone wanted to get in. Fresh fear overtook her.

Beside her, Mick sprang up, instantly alert, his

hand on his holstered gun. He moved toward the door, motioning Bitsy to the far wall, out of range. She followed his silent instruction. He pressed his eye to the peephole and in a second his stance eased. He stepped back, his hand relaxing on the gun, and opened the door.

A petite woman Bitsy judged to be late forties to mid-fifties stepped into the room and embraced Mick. He kicked the door closed and wrapped his arms around her in a protective gesture, dropping a kiss on the top of her head. The woman tipped her head back and studied him.

"You look like crap," she said in the most elegant voice Bitsy had ever heard. Its tone brought to mind the adjectives upper-crust and ruling family. Her ex-mother-in-law had attempted a similar effect, but had always sounded, at least to Bitsy, like someone who needed a colonic.

"And you, as always, Francine, are gorgeous."

"You bet your bony ass I am," she said in that tone normally reserved for asking the butler to serve tea. "Work like a damn dog at it, too." She looked past Mick to Bitsy still standing at the far wall, watching the exchange. "My, my." She smiled broadly. "You don't look like a hooker."

"I'm—"

"I know who you are, darling." Before Bitsy could finish, the woman released Mick, walked over and wrapped her arms around Bitsy. "I'll bet you're scared as—" She filled in with an expletive.

"Francine finds profanity freeing," Mick said.

"He can be a son of a bitch," she said soft enough for only Bitsy to hear. She brushed back the hair from Bitsy's face in a way that reminded Bitsy of her mother, who had been dead seventeen years. "But when the battle begins, you'll want him on your side and be—" she swore again "—glad he was."

The diminutive woman let go of Bitsy and turned to Mick. "It's the old dichotomy really. The old 'don't judge a book by its cover' shtick that makes me fond of socially unacceptable expressions. Plus I've always had a potty mouth. At my age, you learn to pick your fights for what really matters. Decorum is at the bottom of the list."

Mick peered out the door's peephole. "Any problems?" he asked Francine.

She smiled at Bitsy. "In our profession, paranoia is an asset." She turned to Mick. "I'm retired." She spoke the word with an edge of sarcasm. "Not brain-dead." She moved closer to the man. "I must say, you look like—"

He cut her off. "I know what I look like. Personal appearance is at the bottom of the list."

Francine released a rich whiskey laugh that made Bitsy think the woman enjoyed a good shot of Scotch and a fine cigar now and then.

"Are you parked outside the door?"

"The gray Dodge. It's solid. Everything else you need is inside." The woman paused, her face sober now. "They killed Arthur." It was not a question but a statement. The words came hard and forced from inside her as if they needed to be said out loud.

"They were aiming for me."

The woman took out a pack of unfiltered foreign cigarettes, tapped one out. "Do you mind?" she asked Bitsy.

"At the moment, secondhand smoke is at the bottom of the list."

The woman smiled, holding the cigarette between her teeth. She lit it, her head gesturing toward Bitsy as she spoke to Mick. "You got yourself a smart-ass. Good for you."

"Yeah, she's a regular ray of sunshine," Mick said, but when Bitsy met his eyes, she saw something new, something rare. Warmth.

"My, my." Francine inhaled deeply. She must have seen it, too. She picked up the empty soda can Mick had left on the table, flicked her ashes inside.

"The manhunt is on," she said. "A two-time murderer and his moll. Hollywood should buy the rights."

"Two-time?" Mick asked.

"They're pinning Arthur on you too, dear boy." Francine coolly exhaled. "Good God, you actually look surprised. They'd probably finger you for Hoffa, too, if you hadn't been three at the time of his disappearance."

Mick's voice was tight. "They didn't have to kill him. They could have let him go."

"Don't kid yourself, bubala. He knew too much.

Just like you. Everyone's expendable. All for the greater good." She dropped her cigarette into the soda can. Bitsy heard a small hiss. "Helluva retirement plan."

"They've let you live."

Francine threw the soda can into a wastebasket, walked over to Mick and patted him on the cheek. "No, they just haven't found me yet. Here's hoping you've got a wham-bam helluva plan. Now go on out and get the suitcases out of the Dodge." She handed him a set of keys, checked her watch. "My ride will be here soon."

She turned to Bitsy after Mick had left the room. "I'm not going to promise you you'll come out of this alive, but I will promise you if you do, it will be because of him. And if you don't, it will be because they took him out first."

Mick came back into the room carrying two plaid suitcases.

"They're Burberry knockoffs but I liked them. If you're going to go, might as well be in style." She stepped toward the suitcases, tapped one. "The disks are in here along with a laptop and a few other goodies that might come in handy. If you need to use the phones, they're clean. And good ol' cold cash." She turned to Bitsy. "I threw some things in the other for you."

"Goodies?" Bitsy asked.

The woman smiled.

"Might as well go out in style," Bitsy said.

"She keeps this up," Francine observed to Mick, "and they'll be recruiting her."

"Over my dead body," Mick said tersely.

"That's a given, darling." She looked hard into Mick's eyes. "He loved you."

"As he did you."

The woman moved into his arms, clung to him for a minute. It was the only emotion either showed. Bitsy heard a phone ring. The woman slipped a cellular phone out of her Prada purse, another knock-off, Bitsy assumed. Francine flipped the phone open, but did not speak, only listened for a few seconds, then flipped it close.

"Gotta go, bubbies." She went to Bitsy, embraced her. "Don't take any—" she swore "—from him."

"Do I look like I'd take any—" Bitsy repeated the profanity "—from him?"

Francine laughed. She smoothed Bitsy's hair. "I would have liked to get to know you."

"Don't have me dead and buried already," Bitsy said with a bravado she did not feel.

The woman cupped Bitsy's cheek, smiling, but something in her eyes changed. "Not you, darling. Me." She released Bitsy. "Okay, ta-ta, you two." She wiggled her fingers in a wave as she walked to the door, opened it and walked out without looking back.

Bitsy looked at Mick. "Who the hell was that?"

Mick moved toward the suitcases, flipped one up on the bed, popped it open. "C'mon. We've got work to do," was his only reply. When she didn't move, he turned and looked at her. "We've got a long ride ahead of us. I'll answer your questions on the way. Right now we've got things to do." He tossed her a small box "Here. Start with this."

Bitsy looked down at the box in her hands. "I've always wanted to be a redhead."

Chapter Ten

They left at dawn. They placed cash on the round table and climbed into the gray Dodge—a raven-haired man with a crew cut in military fatigues and aviator sunglasses and a pregnant woman with a cap of auburn hair.

"Is that really necessary?" Bitsy had asked when Mick had first held up the bulbous latex form by the straps.

"We have a long drive ahead of us. They're looking for an assassin and a hooker," Mick replied. "Not a grunt and his pregnant wife."

Reluctantly, Bitsy wiggled her arms through the contraption's straps and fastened it across her waist. She shifted side to side, trying to center the latex bulge in line with her navel. She slipped on a pink pin-striped sleeveless maternity dress over her head. In the bathroom mirror, she ran her fingers through her newly shorn hair, taking in its new length. She patted on the concealer from the makeup case across her bruises on her face, applied foundation, mascara and finished off with powder. She gathered the supplies and went out into the other room.

"Here." Mick thrust a purse at her. She opened the wallet inside, to find an Idaho driver's license with a head shot of her with her new hairdo and her face.

"Digital photographs altered with a computer program," he explained.

"Ms. Lorraine Heywood," she read the name on the license. "I suppose you're Mr. Heywood or did I insist on keeping my own name?"

"You wanted to. I wouldn't let you. I'm an old-fashioned guy."

"I wear glasses and have a bit of an overbite in this photo," she pointed out.

Mick picked up wire glasses and a small plastic case. "Put these in your purse. They'll only be necessary when we stop or if someone stops us."

Bitsy unsnapped the case. Inside was what looked like a dental implant of front teeth.

"We've been married six months."

"Can't I just once be a respectable girl?" Bitsy patted her very pregnant belly.

"At least, I made a respectable woman of you."

"You and my daddy's double barrels."

"I'm on leave before I ship out for Iraq. We never had time for a proper honeymoon so we drove to Reno for a wild weekend and are driving back home." He shut the suitcases, picked them both up.

"Is all this really necessary?"

"It's a precaution. Let's go."

"One question."

He waited.

"What's your name this time?"

"Jackson. Jackson Heywood."

She patted her rubber stomach. "What about the little bun here? Have we picked out any names yet?"

"No." Mick walked out. Bitsy picked up Lorraine's purse and followed. The trunk had a false bottom. Mick put the two suitcases in there, closed it, took another suitcase from the back seat and put it in the trunk. They pulled out of the motel parking lot and headed northeast.

"Where are we going?" Bitsy asked.

"Some place safe."

"Does such a place exist?"

"It exists."

"What are we going to do there?"

"I'll review the information Francine got for me and hopefully find out why the Agency was ordered to take out Kittredge. Then I'll ask for a meeting."

"A meeting with whom?"

"With the right people."

"Who would that be?"

"I won't know until I have a chance to look at Francine's files."

"If you're tired of driving, I can take a turn," Bitsy offered.

"I'm fine." He added, "Thank you."

She looked at him in the pale morning light. "You don't trust me, do you?"

"As much as you trust me."

She stared out the window. "I trust you," she said quietly.

He glanced at her. "Don't." His voice was hard. "Don't trust anyone if you want to stay alive."

She was silent, watching the road. "You promised you'd tell me who Francine is."

"She is—was—a member of the Agency. A special operative. Her expertise is computers. She's the best code breaker in the business and she can find out anything about anyone or any operations."

"So she brought you information?"

"She got me what she could, but if she had found the answer, she would have told me. It will be up to me to see if there's a connection. To see who wants me and Kittredge dead."

"Then you'll ask for a meeting?"

He nodded.

"And now Francine is retired?"

His mouth quirked into a contemptuous smile. His new, severe cut only served to make his strong, hard features more prominent, larger-than-life. The black hair, no more than a shadow since it was shorn so close to the scalp, partnered well with the deep blue of his eyes. The changes had made him more devastating and dangerous-looking.

"No one 'retires' from the organization. Primarily because many don't live that long. The ones who do know too much and are too valuable to let go. They may not go out into the field anymore but they work behind the scenes, coordinating operations, manning surveillance sites. Some agents just disappear."

"Disappear? What do you mean?"

"Their identities are erased, new ones created. A whole new life. Past, present and future."

"Is that what happened to Francine?"

"Yes, but not through Agency channels. She engineered her own disappearance."

"Why?"

"After the last presidential election, a new director was put in charge of the Agency. Andrew Corbain. It's not unusual. Simple political maneuvering. Except the Agency began to change under Corbain. Protecting the American people seemed to become secondary to protecting political reputations. Francine saw the shift and it scared her. She wanted out, but you don't just hand in your two-weeks' notice. Then, one day, she was gone. Months went by. The Agency's official word was her identity had been compromised and she was killed by Middle Eastern enemy agents. Then one day, I got a message. 'I'm—'" Mick inserted a swear word "'—okay.'" He fully smiled then but only for a brief second. "And I knew she was. They were looking for her, but they hadn't found her yet. In the meantime, they'd erased her identity, made sure she would never hold a normal job, live a normal life again."

"Why did she contact you?"

"We were very close. And we had a mutual friend."

"Arthur?"

Mick nodded.

"She loved him?"

Another nod.

"Did he love her?"

"Madly," Mick said, his eyes on the road.

"But they were never together?"

"There were moments, yes, for both of them, but not enough. This is too dangerous a business to care about someone. You care about someone, you make yourself vulnerable. More importantly, you put the other person at risk."

"Did she ever get in touch with Arthur after she left?"

Mick shook his head. "He was too close to the top. He was grateful to know she was alive."

"Why didn't he look for her?"

Mick smiled. "That would have really pissed her off. Not to mention put her in jeopardy. Arthur understood why she left, maybe even had moments himself when he wondered if he should join her, but he also believed in the Agency, what they—we—had accomplished. You had to or you wouldn't be able to do your job effectively. A man who did not believe in what he was doing was no more than a robot. And no matter what kind of political whitewashing went on through Agency operations, we were still doing good work."

"But Arthur helped you."

"And was killed for it," Mick said softly. "Corbain had begun to sacrifice his own people. Arthur could not live with that. And then he became one of the sacrificed. Corbain was sending a warning to other agents."

"What about you? What do you believe?"

Mick swept her with a sharp glance. "I believe whoever tried to kill Kittredge and then engineered the assassination attempt to finger me is still out there, walking free. No one, not you or I or Kittredge, is safe until we find that person."

"Then what?"

He shot her another tight glance. "What do you mean?"

"Do you 'disappear'? Like your friend Francine?"

He held her gaze a second too long. "Yes."

For a minute the car was quiet. Then Bitsy patted her stomach. "And who's going to take care of Jackson here?"

Mick laughed softly and sadly.

For hours they drove the rural roads properly maintained but far from the sleek, quicksilver ride of the interstates. They continued northeast, crossing into Idaho and long, large stretches of farmland and little else. The towns they passed through were small, spread out, with no more than a store or two, a post office and a gas station that served as the social center. Bitsy read their names aloud on the signs and insisted Mick play the alphabet game with her, using road signs to see who could find in order all twenty-six letters of the alphabet first, a diversion that made Mick smile when he definitely didn't want to. They stopped for lunch at a roadside diner and, outside of the fact they obviously weren't locals, attracted no attention.

Back on the road, with her stomach full and the tedium of the long drive mounting, Bitsy's head began to nod until she finally succumbed to sleep. Mick was left with the hum of the engine and thoughts better left unexamined. He looked at the woman sleeping beside him. She had curled her feet up under herself, shifted to the side, facing him, to adjust to the bulk of her false belly. He turned away, the sight disturbing and desirous. After Lisa's death, he had never longed again for a wife, a child, a family. The Agency, Arthur, had been his family. Now that was gone, too. There had been women, but they'd been no more than a physical need, a temporary release of basic urges. No relationships. No desire other than physical. No other woman than Lisa had been able to touch him beyond sexual satisfaction.

Bitsy. The name made him smile. He looked at her, liked the new color of her hair, the innocent peach blush applied to her cheeks, the pink gloss of her lips making them fuller, moist. He turned his gaze back to the road. He would make sure she was safe. Then he would go.

SHE WOKE TO PROMISE OF NIGHT against white aspens and the distant purple-blue cast of the mountains, and for a moment, forgot how she had come to be here and just breathed.

She turned to the man beside her. His face was gray in the dusky light, his eyes shadowed but hard and focused. "How long can you go without sleep?"

"As long as it's necessary."

"How do you do it?" She stretched her body, easing the knot between her shoulders. She unfolded her legs. Her hamstring, improved by the long hours of rest, reacted with only a slight twinge of pain. "Do they train you guys? Put you through some secret-agent boot camp complete with decoder rings and poison-ink pens and days of physical and mental deprivation until you're an elite spy machine?"

He pulled into a gas station beside a pump, turned off the engine.

She twisted toward him, her body stretched out along the seat. Her hair was tousled, her face still soft with sleep. She smiled.

He reached for the keys and her hand reached for him, resting gently on his forearm, her fingertips moving lightly across his skin. He looked up from her hand to her face. Her lips tilted upward, parted, inviting. "Is that what you are, Mick?"

Her fingers moved up the length of his arm to the back of his neck. Her chin tilted toward him. "A machine?"

Foolish, he thought, even as his head lowered to hers in response. *Wrong.* His mouth found hers and there was no more thought. Only heat. Desire. Hunger.

She wrapped both her arms around his neck, bending her head back, offering herself freely. The lips she thought hard were surprisingly soft against hers and persuasive. She opened her mouth wider. His tongue moved deep inside, exploring, challenging. She drew him in, desire building, causing her to clutch his shoulders and try to hang on. It was no use. She was falling, swept away by sensation and an overwhelming dominant male sexuality she had never experienced before.

He broke it off slowly, painfully. She was not ready for it to end. He had not touched her except for his mouth, yet every inch of her felt possessed. As his lips left hers, her hand involuntarily fell to his forearm once more. She grasped his wrist, as if to say, "Don't go."

He held her gaze, desire in the hot blue of his eyes. "Does that answer your question?"

He moved away from her touch, out of the car and unscrewed the gas cap. He concentrated on the click of numbers on the pump as the tank filled. He shouldn't have done that. It was a mistake, and he couldn't afford to make a mistake. Emotion, attachment would cloud his effectiveness, interfere with the tasks to be completed. Physical need was one thing and easily satisfied. Emotional involvement was another matter and something he avoided. He finished filling the tank, screwed on the gas cap and went inside to pay. He didn't look at her when he got back into the car, started it up and headed back to the roadway.

Bitsy tapped her fingertips against her lips. "I'm sorry."

She took him off guard again. "You're apologizing?"

"I insulted you. I know you're a man. Christ, I'd have to be deaf, dumb and blind not to."

His laughter filled the car, easing away the unspoken tension. "So now you flatter me?"

She sighed. "How much longer until we get where we're going?"

"Not long."

She settled into the seat, folding her arms across the false bulge of her abdomen and did not speak. They had crossed into Oregon while Bitsy had slept and into the mountains. An hour later, Mick turned off onto another rural road and then eventually onto nothing more than a rutted path overgrown with weeds that would be easily missed if someone wasn't looking for it. They climbed upward, bumping along the path's sharp curves. They crested a small rise. Through the trees, Bitsy saw a clearing. A two-story log house stood in its middle. Mick pulled up to an adjoining garage.

"Who does this belong to?"

"Me," Mick said.

"You live here?"

"Occasionally."

Leaving the engine running, he got out of the car, punched buttons on a small rectangular box on the side off the garage. Grasping the handle at the bottom of the garage door he pushed it up. When the door was open, he got back in the car and drove it into the garage. He got out and pulled down the door behind them, bathing them in gloom. In the gray light, Bitsy saw a motorcycle.

He opened the driver's door. "Wait here a minute while I get the generator running." He slammed the door, went out a side door, and a few minutes later came back and went straight to the trunk. He took out all three suitcases.

"I can carry one," Bitsy offered as she rounded the car.

Mick smiled. "Not in your condition. Come on inside." Hefting the suitcases, he moved toward the side door and Bitsy followed him. Out in the open, he scanned the surroundings. At the house's door, he set down one suitcase, pushed another series of buttons on a keypad. Bitsy saw a green light flash just as Mick opened the door. "Stay behind me," he ordered.

Just inside the door, he stopped, set down the suitcases. "Wait right here." His hand on his gun, he moved into the house. A few minutes later, he returned. "Come on in."

She stepped into a galley kitchen that opened to a large, high-ceilinged room. A stone fireplace with a large, modern canvas above the rough-hewn wood mantel filled one wall. A desk with a computer sat in front of a window that opened out onto the wilderness and the mountains beyond. Most of the furnishings had been draped with clear protective plastic. Mick drew the coverings off as he passed, dropping them on the floor to be taken care of later.

"There's a bedroom upstairs and one down here off to the left. I'll sleep downstairs. You take upstairs." He set down one bag and disappeared into the bedroom with the other two. When he returned, Bitsy was standing by the couch facing the fireplace. Two armchairs with ottomans and a square dark maple coffee table and two smaller end tables completed the grouping.

"I'll show you your room." He moved toward the stairs leading to the second landing. At the top, an open balcony looked down into the living room. She followed him up the stairs and into a large bedroom that extended almost the whole width of the house.

"There's a bathroom with a shower in there." Mick pointed to an adjoining door. "Towels are in the vanity under the sink. There's a toilet and sink downstairs but there's only one shower."

"This must be your bedroom."

"It's where I sleep when I'm here."

"I don't want to kick you out of your bed. I can sleep downstairs."

"No." He headed out of the room, ending any further argument. "I want to be on the ground floor."

Just in case they had visitors, Bitsy filled in the blanks. She crossed the room into a bathroom, which was two thirds the size of the bedroom and included a vanity that stretched along one wall and a walk-in shower beside an oval sunken tub.

"I've died and gone to hostage heaven," Bitsy murmured as she circled the room. When she heard someone behind her, she spun around and found Mick.

"Sorry." He set the vanity case, which had been packed in one of the other suitcases, by the sink. "I didn't mean to startle you."

"No, it was my fault. I was blown away by this bathroom. It's great, but I bet everyone tells you that."

"I've never brought anyone here." He snapped open the small case, lifted its top.

"No one? Why not? It's such a great place."

"In case of a situation like this."

"You built this as a hideout?"

"Essentially. It's got state-of-the-art security systems and everything runs on a massive generator out back. Self-contained. Cut off from the world."

"You come here only when you're in danger?" Bitsy questioned.

"No, not always. There are lots of reasons to hide. Danger is only one of them."

He raised his gaze from the suitcase. "Looks like Francine tried to think of everything." His hand came up from the suitcase. It was holding a gun. Bitsy froze.

"Have you ever shot a gun?" he asked.

She looked up from the handgun he held, pointed not at her, but at the floor, and released her breath. "No."

"You should learn. It's a big, bad world out there."

"Tell me about it." She gave him a tight smile.

His own expression stayed stern. "Francine packed all the necessities. I wasn't sure of your size. I told her small."

"You were wise."

He held up a medicine container. "For your pain."

She shook her head. "The leg isn't bad. Staying off it all the time we drove seemed to help. Either the pain lessened or my body's just gotten used to it. I'll give it a long soak and see."

He set the bottle on the nightstand. "I'll leave these here in case you need them. I know it's early but I'm beat. I'm going to grab some sleep before I get to work." He started toward the door.

"Are you going to teach me?"

He stopped and glanced over his shoulder at her. "Teach you what?"

She dropped her gaze to the gun dangling from his hand. "To shoot a gun."

"No." He turned back to the door.

"Why not? Don't you trust me?"

"Don't take it personally." He stopped, looked at her again. "Don't be afraid. You're safe here. No one can hurt you." With that he left.

Bitsy walked over to the door and closed it. She would like to believe him, but the past forty-eight hours had taught her otherwise.

She locked the door. Returning to the bed, she sat down and rummaged through the suitcase. The clothes were nondescript—jeans, beige chinos, T-shirts and polos in neutral colors. The toiletries in the vanity case were similar to the basics she'd gotten at the campground. It didn't matter. Bitsy would never take even something as simple as a toothbrush for granted again.

She gratefully stripped off the maternity dress and latex undergarment and hung them up. She plugged the tub and turned the faucet knobs on. From the suitcase on the bed, she selected a pair of tan pants and a navy blue T-shirt and laid them across the comforter. In a side pouch, she found delicate white lace panties and a bra to match. She smiled. Francine obviously had decided she didn't need an entirely practical wardrobe. She headed back to the bathroom, humming.

Ninety minutes later, she emerged from the room, wrapped in an oversize towel. The thick steam wafted out from the bathroom into the bedroom, scenting the room with the clean smell of soap and shampoo. She unwrapped the towel around her head, shook free her hair and sat on the edge of the bed to comb it. The pads of her fingers and toes were white and wrinkled from the long soak, but the throbbing in her leg had all but disappeared and the swelling in her face and her thigh had subsided. Bitsy slipped on the frilly undergarments. The bra was snug, her breasts swelling over the scalloped edges of the lace cups, but the panties, cut high on the thigh, fit well.

She dressed and fluffed her hair with her fingers as she headed into the bathroom. Wiping away the steam clouding the mirror, she leaned in, giving herself a critical appraisal. Her nose was slightly misshapen but the swelling had lessened even more over the last twenty-four hours and the gray smudges below her eyes were gone.

She went downstairs and saw no sign of Mick. His bedroom door was closed, so she assumed he'd finally fallen asleep. In the kitchen she inspected the cupboards where she found canned staples and juice, but little else. The refrigerator was not even turned on. Uncertain how long this respite would last, she did not plug it in.

She moved to the living room, settled in one of the sofas, but, restless, got up, circled the room, stopped in front of the windows, staring out but not really seeing the surroundings. She turned away and moved to the computer. She glanced over her shoulder as she sat down at the desk but didn't hear anything from behind the closed bedroom door off the main living area.

She turned on the machine, waited while the system booted up. The log-in screen came on, asking for a password and user name. She hit Cancel but the screen popped back up again. She swore under her breath.

"Did you expect otherwise?"

She whirled in the chair. Mick stood in the bedroom doorway in denim shorts and nothing else. He leaned against the door frame, his arms crossed over his bare chest.

"Don't you think you've given me enough freakin' heart attacks?" She averted her eyes from the sleekly muscled chest that tapered to flat abs and a narrow waist. "Stop sneaking up on me like that."

He contemplated her, infuriatingly cool and handsome with a hint of amusement in his normally hard expression.

"Did you sleep?" she asked.

"Like a baby."

"Bull."

Now he smiled openly

"It hasn't even been two hours."

He shrugged, pushing off from the door and moving toward her. "Give me a couple hours and I'm good to go."

She wheeled back a few inches in the chair as he approached. The chair hit the desk, stopping her. He leaned over her, his arms on either side of her supported by the desk. His gaze moved over her face critically. He bent closer, examining where the punch had landed. She didn't breathe, the electric connection between them heightened by their bodies being so close but not touching. Satisfied, he straightened and stepped away.

"You look better," he said as if she cared what he thought.

"You need a shower."

"I know. Get up."

"You're also too bossy," she added, annoyed by the effect he had on her.

"So you've mentioned. How's your leg?"

"Don't try to sweet talk me," she said as she got up from the computer.

He sat down, typed in a user name and password. A desktop screen with several program icons loaded.

He pushed back. Bitsy, who had been watching over his shoulder, stepped aside. He went into the bedroom, came back several minutes later with a device the size of a cigarette lighter. He plugged it into a port on the CPU, clicked on a drive and waited for it to load. Files began to fill the screen.

"What's all this?"

"Stories, photos, anything related to Kittredge in the last six months."

"You know, my lawyer friend, Grey, he knows someone who works for him. Says he's the real deal."

"Maybe that's why someone wants him dead."

"Maybe, but why do they want you dead?"

She had been leaning over his chair, trying to read the file names on the screen. He looked up. Suddenly she found his gaze on her, his lips incredibly close.

"Because I'm the real deal, too, darling."

Chapter Eleven

Bitsy brewed coffee and sat a cup, black, beside Mick's elbow.

"Thanks," he mumbled, not looking up from the computer screen. It was after midnight. He had sat at the computer since he'd awakened, with one hand eating the sandwiches Bitsy had made him, his other hand steering the mouse through file after file. Bitsy went back to the couch, setting her mug on the coffee table. She curled up on the cushions and tried to concentrate on the bestseller she'd selected from the bookcase, but her attention wandered. Restless, she got up, moved back to where Mick worked.

Looking over his shoulder, she stared at the lists of numbers he scrolled down. "What's all that?"

"Phone records. Incoming and outgoing calls from Kittredge's office, cell and home." He minimized the file and opened another in a new window. "These are his staff members." He clicked on a number. Dialogue filled the screen. "This is the actual conversation."

"Jeez Louise, they tapped his phones?"

Mick leaned back in the chair, rubbed his face with his hands, picked up his coffee mug. "They tap whoever they want. Domestic, foreign. Cellulars, pagers. Any computer geek can do it. Relays pick up ground calls as they're fed into the cables. Digital is an underground analyst's dream. The more technology, the easier it is for Big Brother to keep tabs on you. The calls are scanned by computers for target words. *Bombs, arms, hijack.* Anything that represents a security risk." He took a sip of his coffee. "It's a brave new world."

"Is that what Francine did?"

"It's how she began. Later, as technology became more sophisticated, she moved into codes. The telephones—that's kid stuff."

Sipping his coffee, Mick clicked open a new file. As he scanned it, Bitsy stood behind him, her hands resting on the back of his chair.

"You never told anyone, did you?" he said softly. He set down his mug and swiveled in the chair to face her. "About the child?"

She stepped back. "You have my phone records?"

His expression was gentle, his tone careful. "Dumont Multi-Media is a huge conglomerate that regularly finances political careers to ensure their own needs are met. Corporations such as Dumont spend millions each year in political contributions, not to mention payrolling lobbyists to ensure any possible bills that would ultimately cut into the bottom line never see the light of day. But they also do business internationally with the foreign markets. That means they must be watched."

She took another step backward, then another. Her hands fluttered and she looked down at them as if she did not know what to do with them. Mick pulled over the metal-and-canvas chair next to the desk. She sat, folded her hands in her lap.

"I know all about the political deals. Partying was Johnny's area," she said. "Thousand-dollar-a-plate rubber chicken dinners and Johnny's photo with the man of the hour. I was the eye candy." She smiled tightly. "I looked good and said nothing, even when some overweight senator stinking of promises and pomp grabbed my ass."

Her smile stayed in place. "I was such a fool."

His smile was soft. "Join the human race, Bits."

She looked past him. "I didn't even know if I was pregnant. I mean I had an idea, but I had always been irregular. After two months, I bought a pregnancy test. But I didn't take it." Her gaze came back to him. "I was afraid. Things were going from bad to worse with Johnny. If I was pregnant, carrying his child, he'd never let me go. At least, not with the child.

"He came in late one night. Most nights he didn't even bother to come home at all. Just rolled in the next morning, showered, dressed and went to the office for an hour or two before he got restless and the whole routine started again. Truthfully, after a while, the nights he didn't come home were a relief. It's the nights I heard him come in I feared. He would have been drinking, revved up, raring to go. And he would be ready to take me with him."

She startled, frightened, as Mick's hand wiped away the tears she did not know she had been crying. She pulled back, embarrassed, and he took his hand away.

"That night you fell down the stairs…" He had read the transcript of the telephone call to her doctor. "You didn't stumble. You didn't trip."

She met his gaze. "I provoked him. He had been drinking. I knew better." She dropped her head. "The bleeding began the next morning. The baby was gone by that night."

"You never told anyone?" He did not touch her again. She was grateful. Even the briefest human connection and she would crumble.

She shook her head. Her tears had stopped. She spoke, her voice brittle. "I was never sure. Never sure if on some level I hadn't deliberately created the whole situation. Then it happened. It was over."

She stood, surprised she was so steady on her feet. "I'm tired. I'm going to bed now."

Mick watched her walk away, her head high, her back straight, not even the slightest limp revealing the pulled hamstring. The urge to follow her was so strong, it took all of the self-control he had cultivated for over a decade not to go to her, do no more than wrap his arms around her and hold her until she slept.

He turned his attention back to the computer screen, but sat for a long time staring blankly, thinking of Lisa and his own unborn child. His hands on the desk trembled, and he laid them on the keyboard, steadying them, and scrolled down the file on the screen.

He would save her. He would save them both.

SOMEONE WAS SHAKING HER. She opened her eyes, blinking away sleep, and focused. Mick loomed over her.

"It's almost three o'clock."

She bolted upright, instantly awake, causing him to smile. Last night, despite her exhaustion, she had lain awake for hours, unable to suppress memories better off forgotten. Finally, she had taken half a pain pill, hoping it would make her sleep. It had knocked her out cold.

"I'll make a fresh pot of coffee. Get showered and dressed."

"You're too bossy," she told his retreating back, but she swung her legs over the side of the bed and headed to the bathroom.

Twenty minutes later, dressed, her hair damp and combed back from her face, she joined Mick in the kitchen. He poured a mug of coffee, handed it to her, poured another for himself. She stirred in sugar, evaporated milk from the canned good supplies Mick had stocked, and observed his drawn features.

"Did you sleep?"

He nodded, sipped his coffee.

"How much?"

"Enough."

"Did you learn anything from the files?"

"No official announcement yet, but Kittredge had been putting together a committee to investigate questionable campaign reelection financing. Someone must not like the idea. With the leak on the arms raid, my guess is it's someone who received contributions from international arms merchants funneled in through legitimate sources. Our operation, if not leaked, would have shut down the arms ring. Once the main players were exposed, Kittredge's efforts could have exposed the link between the enemy arms merchants and the source of their generous campaign contributions. Someone owed a big debt to 'the Asian connection,' as Kittredge refers to them. And the IOU was called in. Two birds…"

"One big, bad stone," Bitsy noted.

"It's just a matter of turning over that stone to see what slithers out from under it." Mick stood, dumped the remains of his coffee in the sink, rinsed out his cup. "When you're ready, come on out and join me in the backyard."

"Why?"

"I'm going to teach you to shoot a gun."

He was standing by a tree stump in the center of the yard, waiting for her when she came out the back door. About one hundred feet away, four rubber tires were stacked in front of a tree. A bull's eye target had been drawn on a paper square and tacked two thirds up the tire tower. A half-dozen empty soda cans were piled beside Mick's feet. In one hand, he held earmuffs and oversize plastic glasses. In the other, a gun.

He handed her the earmuffs and safety glasses. "Put these on."

She did as she was told, eyeing the gun in his hand. She had seen it before, watched it blow a man's kneecap to bits. She reached out for it.

"This is a .22 caliber semiautomatic." It was small, as if made for a female hand.

"The long guns, the bolt-action sporting rifle, the pump .22, the M-16 aren't your preference. Hunters, assassins, professionals, yes, but even then, if you're in the bathroom with your pants around your ankles and the Sunday edition and your weapon is leaning up against the kitchen wall in the corner, well…" His thumb and forefinger made a silhouette of a gun, and he fired. "Goodbye, good times."

"Lovely image," Bitsy replied, wetting her dry lips.

"It makes the point." He hefted the gun in the palm of his hand as if the solid, cool weight felt good. "Now, a small gun, a pistol, you can always carry." He finally handed it to her, snout pointing down.

She wrapped her fingers around the weapon, testing its weight as he had, feeling the cool solidness, and she understood. "And so, the name handgun." She smiled. "I'm a quick study."

"You're a smart-ass is what you are." But he

smiled. "The long guns are good for sport. The small guns are best for self-protection." He pulled out another handgun tucked in his waistband. It was larger, heavier.

"This is a .38 Special. Bigger caliber. The larger the caliber, the heavier the bullet, the faster it travels, the more the recoil."

He picked up one of the empty cans, thumbed off the gun's safety, tossed the can where the land sloped toward the path that circled and rose to the house. He shot it five times in four seconds, the can bouncing and flipping wildly down the slope until he stopped, slipped the safety back on.

She breathed in the burning powder smell. "Show-off."

He smiled. "Your turn. Leave the safety on. Never put your finger on the trigger until you're ready to shoot. Stand sideways so you're less a target, plant your feet, extend your right arm toward the target, use your left to support your right. No, like this."

He moved in behind her, his arms rounding her body, adjusting her hold. The clean smell of soap mingled with the acrid burn of gunpowder. His hands came up and covered hers on the gun. "Grip it securely. Wedge it between your thumb and index finger."

His body wrapped around hers. She felt the hardness of the gun, the hardness of the man. She tried to concentrate.

"There are four secrets to good shooting. Hold the pistol still. Really still." His hands tightened on hers.

His thighs pressed against her legs, his body cradling hers. "Maintain sight alignment. You want to align this first sight here—" he tapped the front end of the gun "—between the two rear sights. Then aim the gun so your target sets right on top of your aligned front sight. Finally, you should press the trigger right through to release without anything else happening to your other fingers or your grip."

Bitsy twisted slightly in his arms. "That's only three things."

"The other comes later. 'The subconscious shot.'"

Bitsy leveled the gun, tightened her grip, looked down the barrel of the gun.

"Don't squint, for God's sakes. Keep your trigger finger relaxed. Find your target."

"Anything else?" she snapped, exasperated.

"Don't breathe."

"Don't breathe?"

"Your arm moves up when you inhale, down when you exhale." His hands released hers, slipped down to her waist and held her firmly. "Ready to give it a try?"

She nodded, bracing her right arm with her left, sighting the stack of tires.

"Bitsy?" Mick whispered in her ear. Her body was so tense, she didn't even shudder. "It helps if you take off the safety."

It took her three tries. She aimed the gun, Mick's instructions reeling in her head, his image projected on the rubber stack. She squeezed the trigger slowly, waiting, tensing. The thrust of the shot, the noise jerked her back. She would have stumbled if Mick's body had not caught her. He steadied her.

"The first time it takes you by surprise. The next time you'll be ready."

"Says you," she mumbled. The heat of his body, the nearness of his mouth, the stir of his breath against her neck fractured her focus.

"Try again," he ordered. "Aim for your target and once you start firing, don't stop. Once the hammer is pulled back from the first shot, you don't have to squeeze so hard."

She pulled the gun up, leveling it with her line of vision, tensing her arms, bracing her body.

"Hold your arms firm but not so stiff or your body won't absorb the kickback." His hands ran down the length of her arms. "That's it. Ease up."

His hands moved up, rested on her shoulders. "Keep your shoulders down. Again," he murmured.

She focused, all her energy, tension, emotion on the target. Her finger squeezed the trigger. This time she was ready for the kickback. Her body met the surge of the pistol with only a slight recoil. Her eyes stayed open. She squeezed again and again, seven times total, until the trigger clicked dully. The chamber was empty and the tire stack toppled.

She lowered the gun. Her body trembled but she smiled.

"I hit it." Triumphant, she twisted, found Mick too close, his hands on her shoulders. Slowly the hands slipped down, moving across her back, settling on her waist.

"Slip the safety on," he said.

She did as she was told. He took the gun from her grip, set it on the stump. They stood facing each other like old adversaries. She stepped into his space. Her hands started at his broad shoulders, sensuously crawled down his spine until they found the gun at the small of his back, slid it out, set it beside the other on the stump.

"Now we're both unarmed."

She stepped back into the circle of his arms. He pulled her close with a restraint she knew neither of them felt. Her fingers moved to his face, tracing the hard lines, the small scar no larger than a cigarette burn above his collarbone.

"How did you get this?" she asked.

"Shaving."

She looked up at him, smiling. "You've got too many secrets, Mick James."

His eyes sobered, a light moving into them she had not witnessed before in this man. Vulnerability.

"Are you sure about this?" he asked in a low voice.

She answered by covering his mouth with hers. She had not expected gentleness. He did not disappoint her. His hands tightened like a vise around her waist as he pulled her against him, his hips pressed to hers, his arousal fully evident. His tongue plunged deeply into her. She met him with equal force, her hands moving quickly, roughly over his body, her tongue tangling with his. His lips dragged across the fine skin of her throat, his teeth sinking into soft flesh at the curve of her neck as his hands slid up beneath the fine lace to her breasts, his fingertips circling the sensitive peaks. She wrapped her arms around his neck, her back involuntarily arching, her breathing shallow as he lifted her shirt, lowered his mouth.

They made it as far as the kitchen. She dragged him to the floor, undressing him as they tumbled, and he stripping off her clothes until all that was left was sheer lace. His hand slipped beneath her panties, thrust into her, penetrated deeper while his thumb caressed her, his mouth moving, teasing a nipple, then gliding upward, fastening over hers, his tongue thrusting, matching the unrelenting rhythm of his fingers.

She clung to him, holding him fast, sensation overwhelming her body. Waves of sweet heat started low, then spiked, carrying her away, but still he did not let her go. Again and again, he demanded. And again and again, her body responded until he lifted his mouth from her and released her.

Still she held him, a raw, primitive need surging even as she thought she had no strength left. Her hips rose, meeting his. He thrust into her only to slowly, painfully withdraw, his strong hips and thighs controlling the motion. Again, the deep penetration, the long, slow retreat. She rose to meet him, hung on, her nails digging into the strong shoulders and drawing blood. Her cries were sharp each time he moved into her, her groans long as he pulled back.

Finally, trembling from the strain, he drove into her, and the climax slammed into them, shattering them both, his voice joining hers in a moan as wave after wave of pleasure surged through them until they lay, satiated, sweating, wrapped in one another's arms.

SHE WOKE TO HIM WHISPERING her name. Bitsy smiled, opening her eyes to find Mick's face deadly grave an inch above hers. His finger pressed to her lips and he shook his head, telling her not to speak.

"They're here," he said in barely a whisper. "We have to go. Now."

She did not ask questions. He shoved at her the clothes he'd stripped blindly off her last night. She dressed in a frenzy, and they ran to the garage and slipped inside. She heard nothing but the hard beat of fear.

"They came up on foot through the forest."

"How did you see them?"

"I didn't. I heard them."

"Thank God, you're a light sleeper."

He cocked his head toward the motorcycle, gave her the good grin. "You ready to go for a ride?"

"How come you always get to drive?" Sex, especially good sex, always made her cheeky.

"You can drive or you can shoot. Take your pick."

"You can't do both, Mr. Secret Agent Man?"

"I can. You can't."

"You're such a show-off."

He straddled the bike, kick-started the engine, looked back at her. "Coming?"

She climbed on, wrapped her arms around his waist and pressed her body to his.

"Keep your head down," he told her as he gunned the engine and aimed for the back door.

"Why?"

"You'll see." The motorcycle's front wheel rose into the air as Mick revved the engine. They hurtled toward the exit, the door slowly rising. Mick's hand left the cycle's handle to curve around Bitsy's skull, pressing her head to his back. She heard the explosion. The bike rocked, skidded on the dirt drive. Mick, both his hands on the handles now, leaned it low to the ground, controlling it. Something hit Bitsy's shoulder hard. Mick felt her jump.

"Are you okay?" he yelled.

"Just get us the hell out of here."

"Are you okay?"

Her head still pressed against his back, she turned her face to the side, squinted open one eye and saw the blood dripping down her arm from the gash in her shoulder.

"I'm fine," she yelled above the engine's roar. "Drive."

"Hang on."

For dear life, Bitsy thought.

The front wheel reared up like a wild animal as

Mick opened the throttle all the way. The cycle shot through the woods. Bitsy looked back. Mick's house was a pulsing mass of orange and gold flames rising to the sky. His job, his best friend, now his house. He had lost everything. Except his life. And her.

The cycle cut through the woods, coming out the other side of the hill to the main road. Mick didn't reduce speed, the cycle bouncing onto the pavement. They took a corner, the bike leaning low, hugging the curve. Bitsy heard a car approaching behind them, coming closer, then closer still.

"Take the gun out of my pants," Mick yelled.

"I bet you say that to all the girls." Bitsy grabbed the gun tucked against the small of his back. Mick weaved the bike back and forth across the lane. A side mirror shattered, and Bitsy screamed.

Mick weaved right, left, across both lanes, the throttle open all the way. Still Bitsy heard the engine behind them closing in. Something whizzed through the air past her ear.

"Okay, it's time for you to show me what you learned yesterday."

"What do I aim for?" Bitsy yelled back.

"Anything."

She twisted, fired off four shots, saw the windshield spiderweb.

"I got the front windshield."

"If it's government-issue, it'll be bulletproof. Try to take out a tire. Pretend you're shooting at it like yesterday."

She sighted lower, shot a round. Mick continued to weave. The van came closer.

"Hang on. We're going for a little ride."

Bitsy felt the bike corner sharply. She twisted around just in time to see the bike heading straight for a side road and a metal fence. A red-and-white sign hung from the entry gate: DANGER. Admittance to Authorized Personnel Only.

"What the—" Bitsy screamed. The bike took flight, skimming the top of the metal fence, landing with a thud that jolted Bitsy's teeth through the top of her head. The wheels veered crazily, the bike wobbling, but Mick held on hard, steered it steady. Bitsy heard the crash, twisted and saw the car's attempt to plow through the gate not as successful. A man jumped out of the side door, cocking a long-barreled gun. Bitsy lifted the pistol, fired in rapid succession. On the third shot, she saw the man stagger back and drop the gun, his hand pressed to his thigh.

"Oh my God!"

"What? What's the matter?"

"I just shot someone."

The man's partner, however, remained untouched, peppering shots that rained around the bike as he chased after them. The bike fiercely wobbled, only Mick's skill keeping it upright.

"A tire's been hit," Mick said over his shoulder.

The bike shot forward, zigzagging to avoid the rougher terrain and the other bullets. Bitsy smelled the sharp odor of gas.

"Jump off."

"Are you crazy?" Bitsy screamed back at him.

"They hit the gas tank, too. On the count of three. One…two…three."

They leaped, tucking and rolling, then scrambling to their feet. Mick grabbed her hand, and together they ran toward the steel barrier, their pursuer closing in as they climbed over the fence only to find the land dropped off to a highway below. The road was steep and narrow, curving down the mountainside, and a rig hauling double trailers was slowly making its descent in low gear.

Mick looked back, saw the raised gun, the man sighting them, his finger on the trigger. He looked down. The double tractor-trailer was almost directly beneath them. The two trailers were soft-sided, the kind that used material for the roof and sides, supported by interior ribbing.

They had no choice. They had to jump.

Mick squeezed Bitsy's hand so hard, she gave a yelp.

"One…two…three-e-e-e-e!"

Chapter Twelve

He pulled Bitsy atop him as they landed, wrapping his body around her and holding her fast. The trailer's material stretched, sagging beneath the impact, forming to their bodies. The steel ribbing bent.

Mick moved on top of her, pinning her body to the surface with his own, covering her from head to toe, as they bounced.

Several seconds later that could have been a lifetime, she felt no more jolts. Only the rush of the wind and the blood pounding in her temples and the warm weight of the man protecting her. He did not move. A new fear gripped her.

"Mick?" She said it again louder, "Mick?" The weight was full, heavy, and her fear rose as she twisted beneath him.

He smiled down at her. "I wanted to see how long I could get away with this position." Then he kissed her until the blood pounded once more in her temples and her body began to hum.

He broke the kiss off, lifting his head, alert. The humming was outside Bitsy now, distant but distinct.

"They must have radioed a chopper." He eased off her. "I'm going to crawl on my belly to where the trailers are joined. Hang on to my ankles and follow me."

He slithered toward the front of the trailer, not even giving her time to protest. The whirring of the copter was louder, still distant but getting closer. She lay spread-eagled, on her belly now, flattened against the flexible trailer top. Her arms stretched out to the front until she was able to grab Mick's ankles.

They moved like that, inch by inch, painfully slow as their bodies slithered along the top. The wind and momentum of the trailer threatened to throw them off as the trucker began to pick up speed on a straight-away, unaware of the two human hitchhikers battling for their lives atop the rig.

At the trailer's edge, Mick stopped, reached back his hand for Bitsy. She let go of his leg, took his hand and wriggled her way up beside him. She looked down.

"You're kidding, right?"

Below them was a triangular structure of metal rods linked to one heavier rod that connected the trailers together. There was nothing else but the unforgiving road. The space between the trailers was no more than three feet. The thump of rotors filled the air, and she looked up to see a silver helicopter appear behind them.

Mick looked her up and down in an assessing gaze. "You're strong enough."

She was afraid to ask. "For what?"

"Watch." He pulled his entire body up to the edge, then dropped over the side, his arms and legs braced against either side of the trailer's steel ribbing, holding him suspended. Bitsy's scream was swallowed by the rising hard thump of the rotors coming closer.

Mick looked up at her.

"Do it."

A spray of bullets ripped across the trailer top, splitting the material. The truck began to move faster, the trailers shimmying with the speed. A bullet tore into the material less than an inch from Bitsy. The top sagged, about to give way.

"Now," Mick yelled.

She thrust her body out and fell, her arms and legs reaching for the sides, buttressing her body between the trailers.

"Start moving downward."

A bullet ricocheting above her head off the trailer's metal corner forestalled any protest. Instead, she followed Mick's example, moving crablike down between the narrow opening while the helicopter swooped in lower.

The truck was moving at a dangerous speed now, the driver, unaware of his extra baggage, assuming the maniacs in the helicopter were shooting at him. The truck took a curve, barely braking. The trailers followed the path, swinging in an arc. Bitsy stopped her crab-walk descent, shifting her body to adjust for the trailer's motion. She looked up, saw a figure leaning out of the copter, sighting down the long barrel of a gun aimed directly at her. She screamed, then everything went black as the truck bulleted into a mountainside tunnel. Brakes screeched, metal on metal, grinding the rig to a halt. The space between the trailers contracted, several tons converging. Bitsy pressed against the walls coming closer, about to swallow her whole.

Mick was beneath, moving toward the rig's connecting rods. When the truck came to a halt with a fierce jolt, Bitsy dropped into his arms, which he wrapped around her, steadying her.

"This way," he said.

They jumped off the truck and, hand in hand, they ran along the passenger side toward the other end of the tunnel, stopping at its end, pressing themselves against the tunnel wall. They looked behind them to the helicopter. It was farther back but low once again, hovering. It must have pulled up in time, barely missing crashing into the tunnel wall. A car moved into the tunnel where Bitsy and Mick stood, slowing at the scene of the tractor-trailer blocking one lane. An SUV pulled out cautiously from behind the rig into the other lane to go around it. Mick stepped out of the shadows, into the middle of the road, waving at the car coming into the tunnel. A businessman pulled up alongside him, rolling down the driver's window. Mick leaned in. "Tractor-trailer broken down in the other lane."

Bitsy slid into the front seat, pressed the gun to the man's temple. "He'll give you five hundred for your car."

"I don't have five hundred," Mick said.

"What have you got?"

"Take it," the man said, wild-eyed. "Take whatever I got. Just don't shoot me."

"She's not going to shoot you," Mick assured the man. He looked at Bitsy. "At least, I don't think she is." A horn honked from behind the tractor-trailer.

"I've got money. Credit cards. A Rolex."

Beyond the other end of the tunnel, the helicopter had landed.

"We only need the car." Mick opened the driver's door. The man jumped out and Mick slid in behind the wheel. He looked at the man through the window. "You have good insurance?"

The man nodded.

"Good. I'll try to see it stays in one piece." He patted the steering wheel. "But I can't promise anything."

Bitsy leaned over Mick to the window. "Thanks."

Mick dropped the car into gear and drove it out of the tunnel, keeping the speed moderate as they passed undetected the two men who had jumped out of the helicopter and were running toward the tunnel's entrance.

Bitsy's twisted in her seat to see the men move into the tunnel. For the first time in what seemed an hour, she took a deep breath and allowed herself to sit back in the leather seat.

"You did good back there."

She looked at Mick. "For a girl?" She teased.

"For anybody."

"I don't know. Pulling the gun on that poor man may have been a little over the top."

"It's a fine line."

She smiled. "God, I could use a coffee."

Mick's smile broadened. "As soon as I put some distance between us and our friends back there."

"No friends of mine," Bitsy noted. "How do you think they found us?"

"They tracked us somehow. I designed the house to be secure, self-contained. In-house generators, no outside lines or incoming wires for hackers to piggyback in on. Still the Agency has resources to technology I probably don't even know exists."

"Do you think they're still tracking us now?"

"I don't know how. Everything was destroyed in the explosion, the cellular phones, the flash drives." His voice slowed. "If a downloaded file had been compromised, infected with a tracer, when active, it could be tracked by satellite." His face turned grave.

"If they could track the file user, could they also track the source of the file download?" Bitsy thought of Francine.

"We have to get to a pay phone."

They pulled in to a mini-mart and parked. Mick got change for the pay phone while Bitsy fixed two extra large coffees from a beverage station near the cash register. She paid for the coffees, watching Mick in the store's security mirror. He was waiting for someone to pick up on the other end of the line. His image, even distorted by the bulging mirror, caused emotions to swell inside Bitsy. No longer fear or anger but something equally strong and powerful. And the last thing she needed to feel at this moment.

He banged the phone down as she reached him. She handed him the coffee. "She wasn't there?"

He shook his head, his eyes dark, ignoring the coffee. "She has a toll-free number she uses to be reached. If she needs to 'disappear,' the number autodials to Green Tree Landscaping Service."

"Is that who picked up?"

Mick shook his head. "I got an answering machine. There was a message."

"From Francine?"

He shook his head again.

"What did it say?"

"'Sooner or later, we find you. It's only a matter of time.'" He rubbed his face, picked up the handset once more, hunching his shoulder to cradle it against his ear, while he dropped change into the slot and dialed.

"Why did you kill her?" he asked when the call was answered.

The male voice at the other end chuckled. "I didn't kill her, Mick. You did."

Mick slammed the phone down, looked at Bitsy. "Let's go."

"Mick?" She put her hand on his arm. He shook

it off. His face had shut down, his eyes ice-blue and unfathomable.

"Let's go."

She watched him walk away from her. Another man she might have pressed, grown angry, argued he was being unfair. But Mick was not another man. He'd seen too much, lived too long, too close to the underbelly. And lost everyone he had ever loved. Conventional psychological wisdom would advise him to talk about it. But the things Mick had seen were the things one did not talk about. She followed him, got into the car beside him.

"Where are we going now?" she asked as they pulled out of the lot.

"I need more on Kittredge. I need to get closer to him. I've got to go back."

Bitsy put her hand on his arm. He did not shake it off this time. "I have an idea, Mick."

They headed to the coast on the back routes, ditching the car in an Oakland shopping mall where they picked up baseball hats and sunglasses, spandex biker shorts and nylon shirts. They took a bus to the beach, changed into the bike gear and rented bikes and helmets.

A coastal bike route branched inland to link to Canaan and other small towns. Mick and Bitsy followed it into the town, indistinguishable from the many bike enthusiasts who rode the route on a regular basis. It was almost dark when they coasted by Memorial Manor. Passing a number of cars in the lot, they pedaled several blocks over, then turned right and down two blocks, then circled back to the large peaked-roof building that housed the variety of vehicles necessary in the funeral process—the van with its stretcher-like carrier used to transport the body to the funeral home, the sedan used to lead the funeral procession, the flower car, the limousine for the deceased's immediate family and the hearse, of course, although Uncle Nelson preferred the term *casket coach*. Bitsy and Mick got off the bikes and wheeled them into a stand of pines not far from the building. They took off their helmets and surveyed the activity at the funeral home.

"There's a wake tonight. Looks like it just started a little while ago. Calling hours usually last two hours. Everyone will be busy with that. C'mon."

She led Mick to the side entrance of the garage. They paused as they stepped inside and closed the door behind themselves, and waited until their eyes adjusted to the darkness. Eventually, the dark, sleek forms of the vehicles came into focus. Bitsy motioned with her hand toward the back of the building and a narrow set of steps leading to the upper floor. "There's a studio apartment up there." She pointed to a door at the top of the staircase. "When Uncle Nelson first started the business, he lived up there. Now he rents it to the apprentices if they need a place to stay while they learn the business."

Mick followed her up the stairs. The door was locked. Mick was already pulling out his wallet to get a credit card to wiggle in between the doorjamb and lock, when Bitsy laid a restraining hand on his forearm. Standing on tiptoes, she slid her hand along the top of the door frame until she found the key. "I know. Not as sexy as your secret-agent techniques," she told him, inserting the key into the lock, "but it serves the purpose."

She opened the door and went in. The place was dark, but Bitsy, familiar with the layout, felt her way to the kitchenette in the corner and snapped on the light over the stove, revealing one large room, the high-pitched ceiling narrowing the walls at the sides.

Bitsy moved to the worn tweed sectional sofa that dominated the room and plopped down. "When we were teenagers, and the place was empty, Lanie and I used to come here."

Mick sat beside her. "To do your homework, I suppose?"

She smiled at him but said nothing as she stood and walked over to the two windows at the front of the room overlooking the funeral home. She peeked through the closed mini-blinds.

"There's not many cars left. Calling hours are almost over. Usually, afterward, the family will linger." She went back to the kitchen, snapped off the light just in case the mini-blinds didn't completely block it out. She sat back down beside Mick on the sofa. "Nothing we can do now but wait."

Mick turned to her, his grin sly. "Nothing?"

"What did you have in mind?"

"I thought we could do a little 'homework.'"

Afterward, she lay in Mick's arms, her cheek resting on his chest, feeling the rhythmic rise and fall of his breath and thinking about her life and when it had all begun to fall apart.

Mick shifted, drew her closer to him. She snuggled into his side. Certainly nothing made any more sense now since Mick had come into her life. If anything, it was worse. Except she didn't seem to mind so much anymore.

"So, did you bring a lot of boys up here to do homework?" Mick smiled down at her.

She slithered her body atop his and looked down, her breasts brushing his chest. "Mick, I'm going to tell you a secret." She leaned in, her breasts pressed to him and her mouth to his ear. She whispered, "When I met you, I wasn't a virgin."

His low laugh moved inside her, and she dropped her head into the curve where his neck met his shoulder and kissed the hollow above his collarbone. He held her even tighter, taking her breath away, his palms moving along the curves and lines of her body, a desperateness coming into his touch now until she rolled off him only to pull him atop her.

He took her again, hard and fast, the violence that played too large a part in their lives inside them now, undoing them, heard in their muffled cries, seen in the scratches on his back where her nails pierced his flesh. When it was over, he rolled off her and drew her still trembling body to him, brushing away the hair from her face, the tears of exertion and pleasure on her cheeks. He could be gentle, and she liked that, too. But it was the raw wildness of their coupling that made her feel triumphant, as if they had both fought a very long battle and won.

"Mick?" Her fingertip trailed lazily along his chest bone to the lean muscles of his abdomen.

"Mmmm?"

"This wasn't supposed to happen, was it?"

"Hell, no."

"And it won't last long?"

He caught her hand, brought it to his lips and kissed her fingertips. "No."

She propped herself on one elbow to look down at his face and smiled. "I'm not sorry." She kissed his lips. Her mouth still close to his, she said, "You saved me. No matter what happens, you saved me."

Perfectly still, they heard a door below open, close. Footsteps crossed the garage. A car door opened and slammed close. An engine started at the same time one of the large overhead garage doors rumbled, rising upward. Bitsy slipped out of Mick's embrace and crept to the window. The pickup van pulled out from the garage, her uncle at the wheel. The garage door lowered, the metal panel shuddering, hitting the concrete floor with a bang. Gwen's compact was still parked in the lot.

Bitsy turned to find Mick right behind her. "Uncle Nelson must have gotten a call to pick up a body. Gwen is still here, cleaning up, making sure everything is set for the funeral tomorrow. She'll lock up if my uncle hasn't gotten back by the time she leaves." Bitsy picked up her clothes scattered on the rug and began to pull them on. "We've got about forty-five minutes."

The light that came on automatically when the garage door rose shut off before Mick and Bitsy descended the staircase. They groped their way to the side door and sprinted across the wide lot to the funeral home. They went in through the back door to the lower level, moving soundlessly down the dark hallway, past the silent rooms. The door at the top of the staircase swung open and Gwen came down the stairs. As she passed the display room with its samples of caskets, urns and burial garments, Bitsy stepped out into the hallway from one of the preparation rooms. At the same time, Mick moved out of the display room, came up behind the woman and clamped his hand over her mouth.

"It's all right," Bitsy mouthed to the wide-eyed woman as she took Gwen's hands in hers and led her out the back exit, across the lot, into the garage.

Still holding her hands, she said, "I'm sorry we scared you, but we couldn't risk you screaming. The place could be bugged. If Mick takes his hand away from your mouth, you have to promise me you won't scream. If you do, you could get us all killed. Do you understand?"

Gwen nodded.

"You won't scream?"

The woman shook her head.

"Let her go," Bitsy told Mick. He removed his hand from the woman's mouth.

Gwen twisted around to look at Mick.

"That's Mick James," Bitsy said.

"I know who he is," Gwen said, taking a step back from him.

"He was a member of a covert government agency that gathered information and infiltrated criminal operations."

Gwen raised a skeptical eyebrow. "You don't say?"

"I didn't believe it at first either," Bitsy assured her, "but when two baboons kidnapped me with plans to interrogate and then kill me, well, I started to give Mick the benefit of the doubt."

"Two baboons?" Gwen questioned. "The papers said—"

"I know what the papers said. The government is trying to frame Mick for the assassination attempt on Congressman Kittredge, and they're manipulating the media to help them. They've already killed two others, one a former member of the Agency, the other, an active operative. They'll kill me, too."

"Why?"

"I'm the only person who knows that at the exact time of the assassination attempt Mick was standing here in Memorial Manor trying to convince me he wasn't a Halloween joke."

Gwen looked dubiously at Mick, back to Bitsy.

"He's saved my life twice today alone. And it was a slow day." She smiled.

Gwen didn't. She looked back and forth from Mick to Bitsy as she digested her friend's story.

"We need you to help us. Will you?" Bitsy asked.

Gwen tipped her head, assessing Bitsy. Bitsy knew what she saw—the discolored skin at Bitsy's wrists, the lingering, faint swollenness of her lower face, the bluish-purple marks on her arms and legs from her tumble out of the car onto the asphalt.

"Are you all right?" Gwen asked.

"Few bumps and bruises, but otherwise, I've never been better." Bitsy smiled.

Gwen once more turned a dubious gaze on Mick who hadn't said a word. "The papers say you were hired to kill Kittredge. That you're a professional killer."

"Then I wouldn't have missed."

Gwen looked from him to her friend. "What do I have to do?"

Chapter Thirteen

The family of the deceased had said goodbye and walked to the waiting car, the widow on the arm of a young man. Within minutes, the funeral procession formed and slowly pulled out of Memorial Manor. As the last car left, the call came in. Gwen picked up on the second ring.

"St. Agnes. Room 413. Someone will be right over." She transferred incoming calls to a cellular phone, got the keys, locked up and went out the back exit to the garage. She pulled the van out and headed south. Several minutes later she parked in the back of the hospital, close to the service entrance with the wide freight elevator. Opening both the van's rear doors to shield Mick from sight, she removed the stretcher for the body while he slipped out unseen into the building.

Ten minutes later, Mick strolled out the hospital's front doors wearing a suit, mustache, beard and sunglasses, and carrying a briefcase. He walked three blocks to a nearby electronics store and, after listening to a five-minute hype from a thin-necked salesman, bought the cellular phone models he needed, cable and a laptop computer. Twenty minutes later, he returned to the hospital where Gwen took him out in a body bag to guarantee he'd get back to the funeral home without being spotted in broad daylight.

An hour later in the studio apartment, he sat hunched over the computer, studying the lines crisscrossed on the screen. Beside him, Bitsy silently read the names labeling the gridlines, recognizing an area in San Francisco.

"It's a street map?" she asked Mick.

He nodded. "Little trick Francine shared with me. I went into the phone, rewrote the source code, connected the laptop to the cellular phone modified to automatically reroute the call, bouncing it between relay stations so it couldn't be traced. Meanwhile, the code rewriting has turned it into a super scanner."

He traced an overlay of other lines crossing the streets. Numbers, instead of names, labeled the lines. Dots appeared and disappeared on the network. "These are the phone network relays. These dots are all current cellular-phone calls on the grid."

He punched numbers into the cell phone. The phone locked onto a signal on the screen. A smaller window opened on the screen. Lines of text began typing across the screen—a transcript of a phone conversation.

"Very cool."

"And very illegal," Mick cautioned. He closed both

windows on the screen. "You have a friend who knows one of the congressman's aides, right?" He typed in a complicated series of commands on the laptop.

Bitsy nodded. "Grey went to Berkeley with him. Tim Stafford."

He picked up a different cell phone.

"What's your lawyer friend's cell phone number?"

"Why?"

"I want to access his contact list, see if he has a number for this Stafford."

"Who might have the congressman's cell phone number?"

"Bingo."

Bitsy recited the number.

Mick dialed. Bitsy heard Grey pick up, identify himself. Mick locked the signal. Grey said hello several more times before he disconnected.

Mick's fingers flew over the keyboard, typing in several more commands. A list of names and numbers began to appear on the screen.

"Beverly Martin?" Mick read the name of a top box-office draw.

"Grey handled the annulment when she got blitzed on chocolate martinis and took off with that Chippendale dancer for a quickie wedding in a Reno drive-by chapel a few years ago. One of his favorite top-ten cases."

They scrolled down the list but didn't see the aide's name.

"What now?" Bitsy asked.

Mick typed in another command. A list of recent calls appeared on the screen with several subheadings. "Let's see if your lawyer friend has been in touch with the congressman's right-hand aide recently recently to discuss your connection to the assassination attempt." Mick clicked on each subheading—Incoming, Outgoing, Missed. Under the three categories, several phone numbers appeared with the caller identified as Restricted. Mick opened up another window and listed the numbers, then disconnected from Grey's cellular phone. He brought up the San Francisco street map, zeroing in on each in-progress call, checking the numbers against those in the list. No matches.

"We could call them, beginning with the most recent," Bitsy suggested.

"Might raise a red flag. I'll monitor the network for a while. If nothing comes up by the end of the day, we'll try calling. Once I have the aide's number, I can access his contact list for the congressman's number and reprogram these phones with both their numbers."

"What about the number you called yesterday after you called Francine?" Bitsy asked. "Why don't you tap into that?"

Mick concentrated on the signals coming and going on the screen. "It's no longer in service. Besides any communication system the Agency uses is more secure than Fort Knox and a hundred times more sophisticated than what you just witnessed here. If their telecommunications can be accessed, they'd already be recruiting the man who hacked into their system. Right now the only other main player in this hit parade, besides you and me, is Kittredge. We find out who was afraid of him and his efforts to look into unethical campaign financing, and we find out who's behind all the fun and games the last few days."

Bitsy sank into an armchair. "Unethical campaign financing? Dig deep enough below any politician's shiny surface, and you'll find a case of 'I'll scratch your back if you scratch mine.'"

"What about your lawyer friend's old buddy's claim that Kittredge isn't like the other politicians?"

"Kittredge signs the man's paycheck. What's the man going to say? That his boss is on the gravy train like the rest of the politicians?"

"Maybe. But someone is trying to take out Kittredge. Along with you and me. For now that puts us on the same side." Mick turned to the computer screen. "The only clues we have are Kittredge's plans to investigate suspicious campaign contributions and the leak on the arms raid the same night Kittredge was almost killed. If we can access Kittredge's calls, we might find the connection."

Mick's gaze locked on the screen. Bitsy picked up one of the magazines Gwen had brought over with some submarine sandwiches and bottled water. She restlessly leafed through the magazine's pages, scanning the headlines and photos. Occasionally, she glanced up at Mick intent on the computer, the light from the screen turning his complexion bluish. They had made love again just before dawn, coming together with the desperation that had overtaken their lives the last few days. A desperation that neither would acknowledge outside of hard, deep kisses, frantic caresses, shattering orgasms, and sleep that caused them to toss and turn even in each other's arms. They both knew, though neither would say it, that whether they won or lost, time was running out for them.

"Bingo." His gaze still on the computer, Mick smiled. "Just locked on to Stafford's cell." He recited a phone number.

Bitsy got up and looked at the computer screen over his shoulder. "Who's he talking to?"

"Some woman. Carla. Breaking their date. He must be leaving the office."

The call ended. Immediately another one began.

"Now who's he talking to?"

"Patrice. Says he's running a little late but he'd be at her town house by eight-thirty."

"What a schmuck."

Mick gave a low laugh. "You could always call up Carla and let her know." He closed the window, opened another and typed. "Okay, Mr. Schmuck, show us what you've got besides dueling dates."

Mick punched a final key. A list of names and numbers again filled the screen. "R.K. Home. California. Washington. Cell." He turned his grin on

Bitsy. The one that always made her knees weaken. "Bet you're even ready to forgive him for ditching Carla now?"

"He's still a schmuck."

"A schmuck who just tuned us into Station Kittredge talk radio. Playing all the assassination hits all the time." Mick punched in a number, leaned back in the chair and smiled as words began to form across the screen. Bitsy noted it was the same smile she had seen after his head reared and his back arched and his body shuddered as every nerve and muscle merged into the sweet release of passion.

It was an extremely satisfied smile.

"But what if, like us, Kittredge fears his phones are tapped? He's not going to discuss anything sensitive over the phone lines."

Mick turned the satisfied smile on her. "Bitsy," he asked with a teasing disappointment, waving his hand toward the words filling the computer screen, "did you think this was it?"

GWEN TOOK ONE OF THE TWO family sedans out for a weekly washing, stopped at Clear Park Nursing Home to pick up some paperwork, then pulled over for a chicken-pesto wrap at Ollie's, parking in the alley to allow Mick to slip out the vehicle's rear door in a long-haired wig, full beard and mustache, surfer sunglasses, straw hat and beach-bum garb. He'd stopped at a drugstore and bought toiletries, including spray deodorant with talc, then continued on to a computer store. His last stop was at a novelty boutique aimed at the teen and preteen set with its stock of lava lamps, beaded curtains and abundant Bart Simpson and *South Park* paraphernalia. He slipped back into the sedan and enjoyed on the ride home the beef curry and double-thick milkshake Gwen had ordered take-out.

There was another wake that evening so it was not unusual for Gwen to be leaving the funeral home after nine and drive into the city to meet a friend's brother for a late dinner at one of the newest trendy restaurants. Mick, stretched out in the backseat of the older model Volvo, waited twenty minutes after she'd parked before slipping out the backseat and taking the side streets to the building that housed Kittredge's San Francisco office.

Gwen had printed the building's layout from the Web site of the real estate broker who rented the offices. Along with the property's prime location, the Web site had advertised the building's secure keypad entry at front and back entrances. Mick, in Brooks Brothers now, moved to the rear, opened the briefcase he carried, took out the can of deodorant and sprayed the pad. He fanned away any crystals floating above the pad, waited three minutes, then took out the palm-size, battery-powered black light he'd picked up today and shone it on the keypad. In the black light the deodorant's powdery crystals clung to the skin oils and shone fluorescent on the keypad—on all but four of the ten numbers. Two, five, six, nine and the asterisk button. He punched them in ascending order, then descending, then began various combinations, pressing the asterisk button after each one. On the sixth try, the pinpoint red light at the top of the lock blinked green. Mick heard a click, turned the door handle and was inside.

Kittredge's suite occupied the top floor of the three-story building. Mick took the stairs. The same model keypad at the building's front and back doors secured Kittredge's suite entrance. Mick sprayed and shone the black light. Three-four-seven. Only three digits plus the asterisk this time. One of the numbers must have been repeated twice. He tried different combinations but the red light stayed on. Still the last combination seemed familiar. He studied the numbers, and something about the seven-seven combination kept nagging at him. Then he smiled, remembering Elizabeth Mary O'Hennessey at thirteen and her tale of how she and the other Catholic schoolgirls would write the number four-three-seven-seven on their notebooks during math. When someone coming up the aisle to the desk viewed the number combination upside down, it looked like H-E-L-L. Used to drive the nuns crazy, Elizabeth Mary had said with pure relish.

Mick punched in four-three-seven-seven. The red light blinked green and there was a click. Mick twisted the door handle and blessed Kittredge's secretary who must have been one of those naughty Catholic schoolgirls, too.

Twelve minutes later, he was back on the street and heading toward Gwen's Volvo. She appeared forty minutes later, shut the car door and sighed.

Mick, sprawled along the backseat, noted the stiff hold of her neck. "How was your date?"

"It wasn't a date exactly." She shifted and pulled out into the light late evening traffic. "It was more an exploratory meeting."

"What's the difference?"

"You pay half the check."

"So, no bells and whistles."

"I just kept thinking the whole time I'd hoped I'd set the TiVo up to tape *The Amazing Race*. Pretty sad when the prospect of sex takes second place to a television series."

"The show probably gets better ratings, too."

Gwen gave a light laugh. Her posture relaxed. "And how was your evening?"

"More successful than yours I'd say." He'd already received most of Kittredge's office computer files from Francine. Tonight he'd installed digital network trackers on all the office computers. The trackers would send digital signals rerouted to the laptop. Any e-mails, visits to Web sites or even a letter typed would be monitored in real time.

After a few minutes silence, Gwen said, "Bitsy is my best friend."

Uh-oh, Mick thought.

"At the moment, mine, too," he told her.

"Then what?"

"I disappear for a living, Gwen. Bitsy knows that."

She looked to the side to switch lanes. In profile, he saw her lips were pinched tight together. She had seen Bitsy this morning. Bitsy had played coy but had been unable to hide the postorgasmic flush turning her cheeks pink and her expression slightly dreamy.

"I'll make sure she's safe. I can't promise anything else."

"Well, that's nothing to sneeze at, I suppose. Might even beat *The Amazing Race.*"

THE MIDDLE OF THE NIGHT was a time for rest, dreams, nothingness. Not page after page of messages, files, phone transcripts. Yet Mick sat in the dimmed light, the computer's glow graying his skin, and read. Bitsy knew he would not sleep until he found an answer or passed out, whatever came first.

She had slept fitfully herself, kicking around the thin sofa-sleeper mattress. She was getting edgy, cooped up in the small apartment, too near Mick. He hadn't let her go out with him. Too risky. She knew he was right, but being right didn't stop the frustration when he walked out the door or lessen the fear she endured until he returned. Even then, he had shared little information with her, provided only monosyllabic responses to her questions. He was deliberately putting distance between them.

She swung her bare legs over the side of the pull-out bed and sat up, wrapping a fleece throw around herself. The nights were cool, the apartment damp above the cavernous garage. She padded over and stood beside Mick.

"Anything?"

He did not look up from the screen. He was scanning newspaper archives. "Kittredge sent an e-mail message tonight to his aide. 'Charlie has an appointment.' Daily editions of the *Washington Post* along with *The New York Times* and the *Wall Street Journal* are delivered electronically and downloaded. I'm checking the stories to see if there's any relevance. 'Charlie' must be a nickname."

Bitsy shrugged. "Could be Kittredge's dog. Maybe it's time for his distemper shot."

Mick's gaze came up. His expression suggested maybe it was time for her distemper shot. She sat down in the chair, folded her arms and crossed her legs. She held his gaze, daring him to say a word. She was feeling peevish and cranky, knew it and hated herself for it, but the mood stayed all the same.

Without a word, he turned back to the computer screen, which really pissed her off.

"You know," he spoke softly before she had the opportunity to antagonize him further. His attention remained on the screen. "Even when we figure out the connection and take it to Kittredge's people, it won't be over. Not for me. The people I work for, they don't like to lose." He pushed back from the table and turned to face her.

"I know," she snapped. They had determined this all before. Bringing it up again was doing nothing to restore her good graces.

"I'll set up an anonymous mailbox. I'll show you how to send a message, using an anonymous remailer, so there's no way to trace it back. If you need me, you can send a message to the mailbox, and I'll get in touch with you."

She spoke as softly as him. "Why would I need you, Mick?" She got up and went back to the bed. She lay down, her back to him. They both knew she would stalk out, slamming the door behind herself if she could. She couldn't. They were trapped together.

He turned to the screen. He understood her anger. He had shut down after last night. Last night, when the nightmares had returned. Lisa, laughing, leaning into him, raising her face to his, only this time, the face became Bitsy's. Bitsy, who, for the first time in twelve years, had made him wish he were a regular man with regular problems—a mortgage, college tuitions to pay, teenagers to try his soul, his hair going thin, his body getting soft. A regular man who could give a woman the life she deserved. A home, a family, no fear. A woman like Bitsy. Sweet, beautiful Bitsy whose face now became bathed in blood in his dreams.

He pushed aside the memory and focused on the screen, scanning the newspaper articles, looking for a connection to Charlie. He slept as little as possible, trying to find an answer. But he also did not want to dream anymore.

He was asleep, hunched over the computer when she woke early the next day, his head tucked onto his chest, his hands still on the keyboard. She had watched him sleep before. Even at rest, his profile was hard and taut. Not that she believed the man rested. He slept, but he did not rest. She resisted the urge to step closer, touch his cheek and wake him to take him inside her, give him one moment when there were no memories, no threats, no fears. Only oblivion.

She took a step toward him. He woke, instantly alert. He eyed her. She stopped, unsure and slightly ashamed for her bad temper the night before. He pushed back from the computer and reached out his hand. She moved toward him, took his outstretched hand. He pulled her onto his lap, wrapping his arms around her and burying his face in her hair.

"Maybe it's not you who needs me," he whispered close to her ear.

She smiled, her cheek resting on his shoulder, although she suspected he was only trying to placate her. Mick was a man who had been trained to protect others…and himself. He had learned to need little.

"Ah, yes." She twisted, straddling him, arching back to offer him her neck. "The alibi."

He leaned forward, his lips finding the long, smooth stretch of her throat and feasting. "Among other things," he murmured.

THE DAY WAS ALMOST OVER when Mick closed the computer screen. "Your lawyer friend?" he said, swiveling in the chair.

Bitsy looked up from the game of solitaire she was playing across the bed. "Grey?"

"Do you trust him?"

She nodded.

"Call him. Ask him to contact Kittredge. Tell him we want a meeting."

Bitsy set down the deck of cards. "We do?"

Mick smiled. "We do."

Bitsy placed the call to Grey's cellular phone, using one of the phones Francine had provided.

He picked up on the third ring. "Grey Torre."

"If there's anyone with you, don't say my name." She heard a pause.

"I'm alone. Where are you?"

"I'm okay. I'm safe."

"Are you? Where are you? Are you all right? Are you hurt?"

"I'm okay. I'm safe," she repeated. "I need your help."

"Anything."

"Your college pal who works as an aide for Congressman Kittredge?"

"Tim Stafford?"

"I need you to contact him. Tell him Mick James wants to talk to his boss. We'll tell him when and where after Kittredge agrees to meet with us."

"Mick James? The man who tried to assassinate Kittredge?"

"He didn't do it. He was set up."

"You believe that?"

"Mick James couldn't have tried to assassinate the congressman."

"Why not?"

"Because at the time of the shooting, he was with me."

Another pause. "He hid out in the funeral home after the assassination attempt," Grey corrected.

"No, he was at the funeral home at the time of the shooting. And I was with him. That's why he came back for me. The people who want him dead also want to eliminate anyone who can contradict their story."

"Are you certain?"

"They've already tried, Grey. Several times."

"If James didn't try to kill Kittredge, who did? And why?"

"That's why we want to meet with the congressman. Tell him, 'Charlie has an appointment,' and now we want one."

"What the hell does that mean?"

"I can't say any more. I'll call you back in one hour. And, Grey?"

"Yes."

"If Stafford thinks going to the authorities is the right thing to do, he couldn't be more wrong."

"What are you saying, Bitsy?"

"Those are the people who are trying to kill us.

I'll call you back in one hour." She disconnected, looked at Mick. "Do you think it will work?"

"We'll know in an hour."

One hour later, Bitsy redialed Grey.

"Stafford said he'll meet with James. Not the congressman. Not yet. Too risky. This is the man accused of trying to take out his boss. If your friend's story checks out, he'll take it to Kittredge, set up a meeting."

"Stafford will meet with us," Bitsy relayed to Mick. "If your story checks out, we'll meet with Kittredge."

Mick nodded.

"Okay," Bitsy told Grey.

"Stafford specified you be there also to confirm you have not in any way been harmed or mistreated."

"I'll be there."

Mick shook his head.

Bitsy nodded yes.

"When and where?" Grey asked, unaware of the silent standoff going on at the other end of the line.

"Tomorrow night. Ten o'clock. At your cabin," Bitsy replied. Mick had suggested Grey's cabin. Secluded, neutral territory. He had no doubt the Agency would have it wired to a transmitter and relayed to a satellite feed in an hour. The lawyer's people would have to get their hands on a state-of-the-art high-frequency receiver, but he couldn't make everything too easy for them.

"We'll be there," Grey said.

"We?" Bitsy asked, now the one taken by surprise. Mick crossed his arms.

"I'm your lawyer, Bitsy. Even more, I'm your friend. Either I'm there or this conversation is over."

"Don't pull the 'big, bad attorney' crap with me, Grey," Bitsy warned him. "I'm thinking of you."

"And I'm thinking of you."

"Too many have gotten hurt already."

"That's why I'm going to be there. To make sure no one else does. And to see that you're all right."

Bitsy put her hand over the mouthpiece and turned to Mick. "Grey says he sits in or the negotiations end right now."

"He does realize you aren't going to be there, doesn't he?" Mick said.

"Stafford says either I'm there in relatively one piece or he walks. And Grey will follow him right out the door."

"Tell them to bring in a few more and we'll have a mah-jongg tournament."

"The same people who are after us are after these guys, too," Bitsy argued.

"That's what worries me. It's too risky. I don't like it."

She smiled. "Sorry, love, but after the last week, this is about as risky as going to church on Sunday morning."

"Bitsy, are you there?" Grey said on the other end of the line.

"I'm here," she assured him. "Okay, tomorrow night, ten o'clock, your camp. Give me the directions again." She wrote them down on the piece of paper she had ready. When she finished, she said, "I'll see you tomorrow, then." She looked at Mick for confirmation as she spoke. He didn't indicate yes, but he didn't shake his head either.

"We'll be there. Bitsy…?"

"Yeah?"

"You're really all right?"

"Bring a box of Scooter Pies tomorrow, and I'll show you."

She was smiling as she ended the call.

Mick wasn't.

Chapter Fourteen

The next day dawned perversely bright and mild. Last night Mick had been distant after the call, but Bitsy would have none of it. One, maybe two days max, once the information was brought to the congressman and a deal struck, it would be over. Bitsy would be safe. Mick would go. She had decided after their rift two nights ago, their time was too short for squabbles. She'd presented her argument to him, point by point, as she'd stripped away her clothing, piece by piece, with painstakingly slow, languid precision. By the time she was naked, he'd come to see her point of view.

Gwen drove them into downtown San Francisco where she parked in a twelve-story, all-day garage. One floor above was the rental SUV a friend of hers had picked up and delivered to the parking garage that morning. She bent down in the front seat as if getting something out of the glove compartment so anyone watching could not see her face.

"You know what to do?" Mick asked her.

Gwen nodded. "You're sure you'll be all right?" she asked the two people lying in the back seat.

"These are the good guys, Gwen," Bitsy assured her.

Mick slid a piece of paper to her. "Gwen, if we're not here by the time you come back tomorrow morning, call this number. If there's no answer, leave a lengthy message and have the transmission traced. Understand?"

Gwen nodded, her eyes worried as she straightened.

Mick continued, his voice firm and commanding. "And if something has happened to—"

"I know what to do," Gwen cut him off, her voice taking on the same determined tone. "You come back." She gathered her purse and keys, looked at them both in the backseat. "You come back." She opened the car door and was gone.

"Wait ten minutes," Mick said after the door closed.

"Did you have to scare her like that?" Bitsy asked.

"I wish I could scare you that easily. Maybe you would be back at the mortuary, safe and sound."

She smiled. "Safe and sound? That's what I thought until a few nights ago." She looked into Mick's eyes. "Sorry, amigo, those days are gone."

They were to take the 101 toward Santa Cruz and then follow highways 9 and 236 up into the Big Basin area. A private road to Grey's cabin branched off not far past the county border. The sun had dropped but was still bright when they left, gilding the landscape and burnishing the sky. Not a day for death, Bitsy thought.

They had not gone far when Mick turned off 101 onto Interstate 580. Bitsy looked at him questioningly.

"I marked out an alternative route last night, so we come in through the back door. Just in case there's a welcome party."

"It'll take longer."

"They'll wait."

Gradually the roads thinned to a narrow ribbon, the car bumping across the rough surface. The sky went turquoise to indigo, then black.

"There's the turn-off." Bitsy pointed at a battered road sign for Redwood Lodge Road. Mick turned onto an even narrower dirt track snaking through the trees and undergrowth. Night had descended. Now, with the sky blocked by the thick trees, the blackness seemed complete, relieved only by the slice of the car's headlights. Mick drove slowly through the thin, winding path as it climbed steadily upward, then steered into a sharp turn, where a burst of light from the lodge's porch greeted them. The SUV rolled toward the other similar vehicle parked in the drive as Mick scanned the building and surrounding darkness for anything suspicious. Grey and another man Bitsy assumed was Tim Stafford stepped out onto the lodge's railed porch and watched the approaching vehicle. Mick steered the car so the two men were caught in the headlight's glare. Neither of them moved.

"Which one is Grey?" Mick asked.

"The tall one in the polo shirt." Beside him was a wiry, medium-height man with eyeglasses and the harried look of someone who had not taken a day off in a long time.

"They look harmless enough." Mick parked, cut the engine, turned off the harsh lights. Bitsy reached for the door handle when she heard the click of all four doors locking.

"I'll get out first, come around the back and open your door. Don't get out until then and stay behind me as we head toward them."

The two men watched from the porch, waiting for the couple to get out of the car. Neither acknowledged the new arrivals.

Bitsy waited for Mick to open the door. She slid out of the car, and as she straightened, still behind the car door's protection, she felt against the small of her back the cool length of steel Mick slid into her waistband. She did not even chance a glance at him, the two men's intent stares on them. His hand on the gun against her back, he leaned across her to shut the door, his body covering hers. He whispered, "I'll take that back in a moment."

They moved toward the two men. She walked a half pace behind Mick, his body shielding her. They stopped at the bottom of the porch steps.

"Hi, Grey." She spoke first, but remained behind Mick who had stretched out his arm as if restraining her.

"Mick James?" the shorter man asked.

"Tim Stafford?"

The man nodded. Neither extended their hand.

"Hi, Bitsy," Grey said. He didn't smile. He didn't move. He looked at Mick. "Grey Torre."

Tim Stafford walked to the first step. "I need to search you."

Mick raised his arms, widened his stance. "Be my guest. I have nothing to hide."

Stafford moved down the steps to where Mick stood and patted him down. Satisfied, he stepped back and looked at Bitsy. "Her, too."

"Wait a minute," Mick said, stepping toward her, his body half-turned, his hand on her back in a seemingly protective gesture. "Is that necessary?" Mick palmed the gun into his hand. He looked at Grey.

"Yes," Stafford insisted.

Mick looked down at Bitsy.

"It's all right," she assured him.

Frowning, Mick stepped aside, slipping the gun into his own waistband as all eyes were on Bitsy.

"Raise your arms, please. Spread your legs."

"Tim." Grey stepped forward. "Maybe it would be easier…" He looked at Bitsy.

Stafford glanced at Grey over his shoulder, back at Bitsy and Mick. "Doesn't matter to me."

Grey moved toward Bitsy. "I like the hair."

Bitsy slowly lifted her arms, spread her legs. "It's meant to throw evildoers off track."

"Very clever." Grey patted her sides, waist.

"Did you bring my Scooter Pies?"

"Two boxes inside." Grey's hands slid along her hips, down her legs. "You know, this used to be my fifth-grade fantasy."

"Mine, too." Bitsy said, "Only it was with a member of Menudo."

Grey chuckled as he straightened. He gingerly touched the light bruise that still lingered on her jaw, his expression grave.

She wrapped her hand around his. "I ran into a fist."

He looked deep into her eyes. "I hope the other guy looks worse."

"He got away, but Mick blew a hole in his partner's kneecap."

"Jesus."

She moved into his arms, pressing her body to his as she embraced him. "I'm okay, Grey." She had surprised him. He almost stiffened before returning the hug.

Grey stepped back. "She's clean," he told Stafford.

Bitsy smiled. "But I've got a dirty mind." She winked at Stafford. She had not looked once at Mick, but he knew. They had set up the signal ahead of time. Grey was wearing a wire.

"Now that the party games are over, can we get on with it?" Mick demanded.

Grey gestured toward the log cabin. "Ladies first."

Bitsy climbed the steps, followed by the men.

Grey reached around her from behind and opened the front door. Bitsy had come up to the cabin for a day last year when Grey had tried to fix her up with an investment banker from Modesto. Bitsy hadn't liked the banker but she had liked the calm and quiet and had always intended to take Grey up on his offer to use the cabin again. However, tonight's particular scenario had never occurred to her.

The cabin entrance opened into a wide-beamed, high-ceilinged room with a stone fireplace in its center. The wood floors were covered with Aztec-print carpets. The deer's head mounted over the fireplace always gave Bitsy the willies, but Grey was inordinately proud of it.

"Would you like a drink?" Grey asked.

They shook their heads.

"Well, I do." He moved to the long side table set up as a bar, turned over a glass and poured several fingers of Scotch. "This cloak-and-dagger stuff makes my ass twitch."

He took a sip, gestured with the drink toward the sofa and chairs facing each other in front of the fireplace. "Sit, and spill your secrets. I haven't heard anything juicy since a client last week explained how a French bikini wax can revitalize a sex life." He took another sip of his drink and sat down next to Bitsy on the couch. He patted her knee. "God, I'm glad you're all right."

Stafford leaned in. "You asked for this meeting, James."

The deer looked down on them.

"Last week someone tried to assassinate your boss."

"According to the press, it was you."

"You believe everything you read in the papers, Stafford?"

"I'd be a fool if I did."

"You don't strike me as a fool."

"Why did the papers say it was you who shot at Kittredge?"

"Good question." Mick leaned back, crossing his legs and stretching his arm out along the back of the sofa. "But I have a better one. Why did you set up the hit?"

Stafford narrowed his eyes as if keenly interested, but Bitsy saw something else there, too. Bemusement. He was not afraid.

He gestured with an outstretched hand, urging like a good host. "Please continue."

"Yesterday it was announced an American businessman, Xiaobo Sheng, was appointed to a White House advisory body, the Commission on United States–Pacific Trade and Investment Policy. Charlie, as Mr. Sheng is known by his adopted American name, is an American citizen and financier with residences and interests in both the U.S. and the Far East. He, along with a Chinese engineering executive, Yhangki Chen, are sole directors of a California corporation, Prime Investments."

"I read the papers, too, James," Stafford commented drily.

"But what you won't read is Prime Investments is an affiliate of a firm in Beijing that shares ownership with another company that is a front for the People's Liberation Army. Even more interesting, Yhangki Chen is the daughter of a top Chinese general in the PLA, whose job is to work with businessmen such as Sheng to make money and build power for the Chinese armed forces by peddling weapons worldwide, including the California street gangs right here in our own backyard."

Stafford lifted a brow. The gesture was rehearsed and exaggerated.

Mick deliberately ignored the taunt. "Of course, before any of this could come to light, the covert operation linking the California arms ring with the Chinese ruling elite was compromised. Records show Sheng, using funds from Chinese military sources, contributed generously to the Republican National Committee along with a variety of election campaigns that put the current administration into power."

"You've succeeded in keeping my attention, James. Well done. But I still don't understand why I would arrange to have my boss killed."

"When the current administration came into power, Andrew Corbain was appointed the director of the Agency of Policy Coordination. The Agency was originally created to serve and safeguard the American people, but, under Corbain and the current administration, its purpose has become to protect politicians. Your boss, Kittredge, was starting to look into some of the same unethical dealings I just mentioned at the same time the Agency was moving in on the arms ring. I played a major role in that operation. I was easily expendable. Obviously so was Kittredge, except a valet screwed that up. Or was it supposed to only be a warning after all?"

"And I'm the mastermind behind this scenario?"

Mick barked a laugh "Good God, no." He leaned in, his hands on his knees. "But you were promised an appointment for your assistance. Did you tell Mom last night when you stopped by for linguini with white clam sauce?"

"You tapped my phones. Computer, too, I imagine."

Mick leaned back. "It's a brave new world, Stafford."

"So you have the files, records, conversations, all the necessary proof."

"And packets ready to go to a variety of Democratic congressmen and senators, not to mention press releases to Phillips Broadcasting, major rival of Multi-Media Industries." He winked at Bitsy. She smiled thinly. "If we're not back in one piece tomorrow morning, the exploits of you and your buddies will be front-page feed for the masses."

"You forget one thing," Stafford said. "We're politicians. We can put a spin on anything."

Mick sat back, propping a foot on one knee, his smile expansive. "The lone, crazy assassin. The female hostage. Two white knights. A showdown.

The bad guy had to be taken out. Unfortunately the fair maiden and a white knight were also sacrificed before the assassin was stopped. When it's all over, only one remains. And America has a new hero and their next candidate for high political office."

"Classic storyline, don't you think?" Stafford deliberately baited.

"Definitely has all the elements," Mick agreed, equally cool.

Bitsy saw the tight smile on Stafford's face. She saw a jaw muscle near his ear twitch. As if watching from a distance, she saw the gun appear in his hand, aim at Grey, then fall as Stafford fell, his head bouncing back against the sofa, part of his face gone. It had all happened in less than a second. She had not even had time to scream. She did not know if she would have anyway.

Grey said something, but her mind didn't register what. She looked at Mick, the gun in one hand. *It was almost over*.

A blast ripped through the room, shattering the lamps, throwing the room into darkness. There was a brilliant flash of automatic gunfire, and Mick lurched, pulling her and Grey down with him. A long burst of gunfire splintered the wall two feet above them. In the ocean of noise and light, with Mick's body on top of hers as they rolled on the wood floor, her only awareness was that they weren't dead yet. A half second later, another burst of gunfire gnawed up the floor where they'd just lain. In the flashpoint of fire, she saw

Mick above her, looking down at her. Then they rolled again, behind the fireplace's stone wall.

"Who'd you tell about this meeting? The local Feebs?" Mick screamed at Grey above the noise, his body still covering hers.

"Yes. But Stafford didn't know. And the feds told me they wouldn't shoot unless they had to take you out."

A rour of shots punctuated the room. "They're trying to take everybody out. It's not the feds shooting at us," Mick yelled back. "It's old pals. Surprise. Surprise." Bitsy could only see the shape of Mick's features in the fireplace's shadow. He was looking down at her as he spoke to Grey. "Call in your cavalry. Tell them to move in in a big way. Announce they came to play. I'll break out the back, draw the fire." Bitsy clutched his sleeve. His gaze never left hers. "The Agency may be messed up, but they're not so far gone they'll start shooting at feds. Gets the guys back at the Bureau in D.C. cranky."

"Mick?" Bitsy clung to him now. In contrast to his demanding voice, hers was barely a whisper.

He brushed back the hair from her face. There was another blast of gunfire. No time left. He lowered his head, his mouth to hers. "If you need me, I will be there."

Her hands fisted in his shirt. "I need you."

He kissed her hard and deep, and she matched his urgency. He broke away, rolled off her and was gone. She lay unmoving, exposed, empty.

She heard the amplified boom of the FBI announcing their arrival. The gunfire ceased. Grey crawled over beside her. "They're moving in. It's over. You're safe, Bitsy."

She could have cared less.

MICK MOVED INTO DARKNESS, staying low, the semi-automatic in one hand, pointed into the night, no match for the larger automatics his former colleagues had brought to the party. He dropped, crawling through the ground cover, blending with the night. He heard the FBI move in, the gunfire cease. Whoever the Agency had dispatched would already have disappeared. Spooks. Still he stayed low, moving away from the cabin, taking the danger with him. He stopped about five hundred yards away, listened. He had not heard a sound when Andrew Corbain appeared before him twenty feet away. He might not have even seen him except for the flash of starlight bouncing off his night-vision glasses. Corbain did not say a word as he raised the rifle with the long, tubular suppressor and aimed it at Mick's head. Mick threw himself into the bushes and rolled, his gun trained on the slightly darker image that was Corbain. The mass moved toward Mick, sighting him in the crosshairs. There was a barely audible pop, and in the muzzle flash, Corbain smiled. Mick twisted like a caught fish, the afterimage of Corbain smiling, smug, burned into his retinas. He pointed the gun, waited for the next flash, waited for that smiling face to be revealed.

BITSY MOVED TOWARD the tank-like SUV, an FBI agent at either side. The night air was cool, but it was not the cause of her involuntary trembling. She was almost to the wide-wheeled, high-bodied vehicle when a single gunshot shattered the night. Her stomach hollowed. Only the two men on either side of her kept her upright. She opened her mouth to cry out but no sound came. Only the echoing ring of the gunshot.

Chapter Fifteen

They never found his body. Only a trail of blood leading away from Andrew Corbain's corpse. A single gunshot had pierced Corbain's heart. The scoped Remington with a silencer lay on the ground nearby. It had been fired several times. The blood trail led investigators a mile into the wilderness to a clear stream where it stopped. The story was released that a shootout between the crazed assassin and government officials had led to several deaths, including the congressman's aide and a government agent, before the assassin had turned the gun on himself and committed suicide.

But there was no body. So every day Bitsy woke with hope.

She did not entertain the alternative, although sometimes, in the quiet, the thought that Mick could be dead, would sneak in. Other times, the not knowing gnawed at her like one of those rare parasitic bugs that ate you alive from the inside out.

Then she would see him grinning, the puckered white scar on his neck stretched tight, hear his voice. "I'm a Siamese, remember."

She never stopped missing him.

A congressional committee, chaired by Congressman Kittredge, convened to investigate questionable campaign funding. There was no doubt Kittredge would win his second term by a landslide. Grey was asked if he had ever considered running for political office. He had not yet given an answer.

Prime Investments shut down, its co-directors disappeared, presumably back to the safety of their birthplace. The official public statement was that the administration had had no knowledge of Charlie Sheng's possible connection to the PLA at the time of his appointment, which was deemed a huge mistake and promptly withdrawn.

A few arrests of Chinese gang members charged with trafficking in illegal firearms were made, but the major suppliers laid low and waited for the storm to pass.

Phillips Broadcasting trumped every major media market, starting with the shootout story and every other subsequent development.

No mention of the Agency of Policy Coordination was ever made.

Bitsy almost deleted the e-mail message when it came. It had been six weeks. She had waited for the image of Mick to fade. It had not. As she sat at her computer, she pressed her head against the phone, holding it in the crook between her shoulder and neck, half-listening to Lanie's latest complaints about her boyfriend. Lanie called late every night, even after they had worked together all day. The guilt, Bitsy imagined, for Lanie walking out, leaving her that morning with Mick. Even though it was not Lanie's fault. The guilt. And the love.

"So," her cousin droned, "when his buddies called, needing another body for five on five, did he once—"

Bitsy readjusted the phone against her ear, scrolling through the spam that, despite the filters and message blockers, seemed to reproduce itself at an astonishing rate. Make a Million-dollar Income Without Leaving Home. Girls! Girls! Girls! Refinance Your Home at Lowest Interest Rates Ever. Amazing Penis Enlarger.

Bitsy frowned. She supposed if she had a penis, she would entertain the idea of having it three inches bigger, but somebody obviously hadn't done their target-market homework. She pressed Delete.

Her finger was still on the button, Lanie's voice still steady and almost soothing with its familiar indignation in her ear, when she saw the message:

To: Ethel June
From: Leslie

There was no subject. Only two attachments. She ran a finger over the names, tracing the letters. Ethel June. Leslie. She clicked on the first attachment. An e-ticket came up. To Cancún. One-way. The date was open ended. She clicked on the other. The same thing, only the departure and destination points were reversed. On each the passenger Bitsy Leigh.

"Hey, Bitsy, are you there?" Lanie asked.

She was not.

She told Lanie and Gwen and Uncle Nelson she was going to take a vacation, but when she said goodbye to Gwen, she squeezed both her hands hard. Gwen smiled brightly as she pulled Bitsy into her embrace, and they both knew Bitsy wouldn't be coming back.

She changed planes and airlines in Houston, the connection tight, the terminals at seemingly opposite ends, but forty-five minutes later, the flight to Cancún lifted off with Bitsy ensconced between an elderly woman with a grandmotherly smile and a businessman who ignored them both.

Two hours later, the plane landed. The heat washed over Bitsy as she walked from the plane. She had packed one small carry-on bag so she did not join the other passengers retrieving their luggage nor those queuing up for a taxi from the mainland to the island. She headed to a service counter and was directed to the far side of the terminal and a brown-skinned, stout man sitting with a sweating bottle of Coca-Cola at a metal desk. He studied her ticket, then her with a thin gaze, before picking up the phone and making a call. "Have a seat, senorita," he said in his heavy accent and an undertone that suggested a disdain for American tourists. He pointed with his weak chin toward two metal chairs nearby. "Dominic will be here as soon as the plane is ready."

She sat straight-backed, grasping her shoulder bag on her lap with both hands. Her carry-on bag stood upright, aligned with her sandaled toes. She stood immediately when the putty-colored, metal door behind the fat man at the desk opened and the Mexicano stepped out. Dominic, she assumed, was tall and wiry and stood with his hand on his hip as he took her in. He smiled, the dark skin crinkling around even darker eyes and the teeth flashing white. He moved to the desk, bent his head and said something to the man in Spanish. The man at the desk looked up and studied her keenly once more, and Bitsy knew whatever had been said was about her. Dominic moved toward her with the loose-limbed grace of a dancer and extended his hand.

"Senorita Bitsy." He smiled and she did, too, her name even more amusing in his light accent. "Finally you come."

Bitsy crinkled her brow. "You were waiting for me?"

The Mexicano showed even more white teeth. "Not me. The senor."

Bitsy's heart skipped.

"You'll see." He picked up her lone bag, glanced around for more.

"That's it."

His smile eased. "You travel light?"

"Can we go? Please?" she asked, unashamed of the urgency in her voice.

His eyes were soft. His smile returned. "Come."

She followed him through the door into a metal airplane hangar. A small carrier plane, better known as a puddle-jumper, waited past the tin building's open doors on the airstrip. Bitsy walked quickly, Dominic smiling all the time at the anxious American. The hinged canopy to the cabin was already up. Bitsy stepped up and settled in one of the two seats behind the cockpit, strapped on the seat belt. Dominic climbed in behind her and, after stowing her bag beneath the other passenger seat, sat down in the pilot's seat and slipped on a headset. Fifteen minutes later they began to taxi down the airstrip.

Once in the air, Dominic pulled off his headset, let it dangle around his neck. Bitsy leaned forward.

"Where are we going?"

"Not far, about one hundred kilometers outside the city, but the roads are dirt and much is thick jungle, undeveloped. No roads at all. Easiest to get there by plane."

"The senor? You know him well?"

"Well enough." Dominic said no more but smiled slyly.

"And he has spoken of me?"

"Not so much with his voice. But with his eyes."

He looked at her. "I make one flight daily back and forth. If there are no passengers, there is always mail, supplies. Every day, I see this man, waiting. I say to Raul, the airport manager, 'Who is that?' Raul says, 'That's the American.' I say, 'What is he waiting for?' Raul shrugs. 'Crazy gringo.' I watch the American. He has a hard, closed face, but when I look at his eyes, I see he is not mean. Only lonely. I think to myself he waits for a woman." Dominic grinned. "He tells me the name. Bitsy." His grin widened and he nodded as if all was right with the world. "You are the Bitsy."

"And the senor? He is well?"

"He will be better now."

Dominic pointed out the side window into the distance. "There is the senor's ranch. The airstrip is a little farther."

Bitsy peered through the window. As they came closer, Dominic angled the plane's nose down. "There is the house."

She saw a high, single-story house of off-white stucco with tall, dark windows. A neat, grassy yard with a stepping-stone walk led to the front door. The house was surrounded by a nine-foot-high wall of the same off-white stucco broken by a simple Spanish gate.

Dominic dropped a wing. "See the gate? It looks like wrought iron, no? It is steel. The bolt is electronic, latest technology, and the delicate leaves at the top of the gate are sharp as knives."

Bitsy met the other man's gaze. In the black depths, she saw understanding.

The airstrip was a one-lane dirt swath cut out of the jungle. A tin-roofed, concrete-block building sat nearby, palm bushes fanning around its bottom. Next to it, a wind sock hung off a high pole. A big steel box sat behind the building, no doubt housing a generator. Past it, leaning against the thick palm tree trunks, stood Mick. He was tanner and leaner than before. His hair had grown in and was bleached white-blond by the sun. He wore sunglasses and loose-fitting pants and shirt. She began to cry immediately.

"You see," Dominic said, looking at Mick. "Every day like this. He is here. Waiting." The pilot turned, saw the tears coming down her face. He laughed, not meanly, but softly, happily.

The plane landed with a bump and shudder, then went still. Dominic shut off the engine. Bitsy was climbing out before the hinged door was all the way up. Mick had seen her as soon as she'd stood and was already moving toward her. They met halfway, stopped to stare at one another.

"You're here," he said.

"I'm here," Bitsy whispered. She fell into his arms with a small, muffled sob so unlike her. They held each other tight, their arms wrapping around their bodies, gripping each other too hard. The first kiss was urgent and desperate. They broke apart only when they had no more breath left. Bitsy buried her face against his chest, her eyes squeezed tight, touching the muscles of his back, his shoulders. Their bodies pressed together, the contours still fitting. She raised her head and found his mouth again.

From a respectable distance, Dominic leaned against the plane's belly, his arms folded, his head tilted. And smiled.